"The last clear memory I have is of you," Tag said.

She looked up then, her soft gaze warm with care and optimism, and the words just burst out from the unguarded heart of him.

"I never stopped thinking about you, dreaming about you. Loving you," he added.

For a moment she didn't react and he experienced a terrible anguished panic. He was too late.

Then she rose from her cross-legged position and came to him without a word. He stood there, frozen in place, afraid to hope, afraid to breathe. Her palms skimmed up either side of his immobile face, cradling him in that gentle V while she spoke the answer that fed his soul.

"Neither did I."

Dear Reader,

Take a break from all the holiday shopping and indulge yourself with December's four heart-stopping romances from Silhouette Intimate Moments.

New York Times bestselling author Maggie Shayne kicks off the month with *Dangerous Lover* (#1443), the latest in THE OKLAHOMA ALL-GIRL BRANDS miniseries. An amnesiac seeks the help of his rescuer, but the bewitching woman might just be a suspect in his attempted murder. Next is Lyn Stone's *From Mission to Marriage* (#1444), the new installment in her SPECIAL OPS miniseries. A killer vows revenge, and as the chase heats up, so does Special Ops agent Clay Senate's desire for his sexy new hire.

In Nancy Gideon's *Warrior's Second Chance* (#1445), a determined heroine must save her family by turning to the man she left behind years ago. But will her secret douse the flames of their newly rekindled romance? And be sure to pick up *Rules of Re-engagement* (#1446), the final book in Loreth Anne White's SHADOW SOLDIERS trilogy. Here, a wanted man returns to save his country...but to do so he must reunite with the only woman he's ever loved— his enemy's daughter.

Starting in February 2007, Silhouette Intimate Moments will have a new name—Silhouette Romantic Suspense, but we will continue to deliver four breathtaking romantic-suspense novels each and every month. Don't miss a single one! Have a wonderful holiday season and happy reading!

Sincerely,

Patience Smith
Associate Senior Editor

Please address questions and book requests to:
Silhouette Reader Service
U.S.: 3010 Walden Ave., P.O. Box 1325, Buffalo, NY 14269
Canadian: P.O. Box 609, Fort Erie, Ont. L2A 5X3

Nancy Gideon

WARRIOR'S
SECOND CHANCE

Silhouette®

INTIMATE MOMENTS™

Published by Silhouette Books

America's Publisher of Contemporary Romance

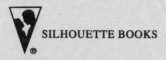 **SILHOUETTE BOOKS**

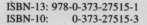

ISBN-13: 978-0-373-27515-1
ISBN-10:   0-373-27515-3

WARRIOR'S SECOND CHANCE

NANCY GIDEON

Portage, Michigan, author Nancy Gideon has a writing career that is as versatile as the romance market itself. Her books include many genres such as historicals, Regency contemporary and paranormal. She has won a *Romantic Times BOOKreviews* Career Achievement in Historical Adventure award, is a Holt Medallion winner and a Top Ten Waldenbooks series bestseller. When not working on her latest plot twist at 4:00 a.m. or setting depositions at her full-time job as a legal assistant, she's cheerleading her sons' interests in filmmaking and R/C flying, traveling (for research purposes, of course!) and rediscovering the joys of single life. Visit her at: www.TLT.com.

For my friends at MMRWA
as proof that perseverance pays off.

Prologue

"Don't go."

Her soft plea held the strength to still his breathing as he reached for his jeans.

"I have to. I have to report in tomorrow. I've got to pack. Besides," he cast a quick glance over his shoulder, "we've already risked enough by you staying out here so long."

Fingertips grazed his ribs, effectively stopping his heart, as well. Her voice became softer still. So sweet, but an enticement nonetheless.

"I meant, don't leave me. Not tonight. Not tomorrow."

He gulped for air to get his pulse and thought process going again while devouring her with a hungry gaze. The offer was unbelievably tempting. Canada was so close, as close as this, his heart's desire. And just as impossible to reach. He stood, pulling up his pants in the same strong motion. Those determined movements didn't give away the wealth of frantic emotions beating him up on the inside. He couldn't let her know how weak he was when it came to her request. When it came to her, period.

She lay on the swing, his letter sweater hugged to her smooth, silky skin, skin still moist from his hurried kisses. She lifted up on one elbow to watch him readying to leave her. Not for just this night, but for countless nights to come. The tousled spill of her fair hair created an angelic frame for her even paler face. Light from the back porch gleamed along the trail of her tears. He reached out to soothe away one of those glittering tracks. His reply conveyed an unyielding regret.

"Sorry, Barbara. Same answer to both things."

A heart-savaging smile tried to strengthen the tremble of her lips, making them all the more alluring. Then she spoke with all the honesty in her soul. "I know. But it doesn't change how I feel. Not about you. Not about us. You can't blame me for wanting to hold on to you just a little bit longer. What time does your bus leave?" Her words snagged at the end of that question.

"Six o'clock."

"I'll be there."

It was no easier for him to say than it was for her to hear.

"I don't want you to be."

Hurt and confusion flooded her eyes, making them into great salty seas in which a man could drown if not careful. He was already treading dangerously deep waters and knew he should just go. To linger only prolonged the inevitable. And hurting her was the last thing he'd ever wanted to do. Especially not tonight.

"Let's say our goodbyes here," he urged, eager to restore the tenderness of moments before. "It'll be better just between the two of us."

Her smile took a bittersweet twist, catching his meaning with a maturity far beyond her almost seventeen years. "Better than in front of half the town. I don't care about that."

"Better than in front of your parents. And I do care."

"People will think it's strange if I'm not there to see the three of you off."

"I don't care what people think."

As long as it wasn't the truth. The truth that a McGee from the wrong side of the justice system and Judge Calvin's pristine, not-yet-of-legal-age daughter were romantically...and physically involved. If that truth were known, he wouldn't live long enough to get on that bus to shake off this town and the stigma his family hung around his neck like a heavy, damning albatross. A reputation he could only live down if he got away, now, right now, before this beautiful, innocent woman-child suffered for its stain. That made him a hero in her eyes, a coward in his own.

She didn't argue the point. That always surprised him, her willingness to just let things go considering that arbitration and critical examination were part of her family tradition. The Calvins loved to sink their teeth into any situation…and bite down hard until they won that point, whether they were right in the first place or not. Blind justice and closed minds. A dangerous combination when it came to courting a rich man's daughter. Courting in the shadows because the honorable front door had always been locked tight for security's sake where he was concerned.

But then he'd gone and stolen their most valuable possession anyway, despite their precautions. Like a thief in the night. That's how he felt at this fragile moment. And he hated it, along with the name that made him so unacceptable.

She sat up, letting the sweater drop, exposing her creamy, perfect breasts without a trace of guile or manipulative intent. Between them, on a slender sterling chain, where it should have warded him off like a virgin-corrupting vampire, was the religious medallion her father had given her upon her confirmation. She slipped it over her head and then reached for one of his hands, turning it palm upward to make a cup into which she poured that trickle of silver. She curled his fingers over the St. Christopher's medal and pressed them tight with both her hands. Her touch was cool, her hands trembling.

"I want you to take this."

"I'm not Catholic."

"God won't care. I don't care. I just want you to have a piece of me with you wherever you go."

Silly girl. Didn't she know she had already carved out a permanent niche within his soul?

"Okay." His tone sounded brusque despite the shaky state of his own emotions. He couldn't afford to let her know how much the gift meant to him. How much she meant to him at this very moment when parting was only hours away.

She released him so he could loop the chain about his neck. The medallion fell against his chest, next to the agitation of his heartbeats, the metal still warm from her skin. Burning there with the heat of their desperate passion. He knew he'd never take it off, that sacred symbol of their love.

"You'll write?" Her question quivered slightly with intensity.

"I'd like to but—"

"I've got a post office box in Roseville so no one will know. Please."

He tried to ignore an angry jab of unfairness at that necessity. So no one would guess what the two of them had become to one another. Loves. Lovers.

"Whenever I can," he promised a bit tersely.

"It won't be like this forever," was the promise she gave him in return.

He'd heard it before. An empty promise made from a pure and painfully innocent soul. One not yet scarred by the ugliness of the society denying them approval and legitimacy in their relationship. Things a girl like Barbara Calvin needed. Deserved.

"They'll change their minds. I'll start working on them the minute you leave and will have them worn down by the time you come home a hero."

Didn't she realize it would take more than a chestful

of medals to outshine the blackness of his past? But because she looked so hopeful, so damned gorgeous in her conviction, he only nodded.

She leaned forward to kiss him. Passion tasted wild and fierce in that long, wet exchange. And when she sat back, her expression was set with a strength that almost convinced him.

"I will marry you, Taggert McGee. You keep that promise close to your heart, too, and you come back for me. I'll be waiting."

So he took that promise with him on the bus the next day, along with a PO box number. He pretended he didn't see her standing at the edge of the curb trying to hide her tears.

He carried that promise through the rigors of basic training while he sent off letters and waited anxiously for a reply. A reply that never came.

And the next time he heard anything about her, just before he shipped out, was that she now carried his best friend's last name.

Even after thirty years, the pain of that discovery was still close to unbearable. Even as he stood in the cemetery glaring down at the name carved into pale marble. A stone as hard as his heart had become.

"You son of a bitch. You were supposed to take care of her. You're the one she should be depending on, not me."

Pride wouldn't allow him to rejoice in his chance to take Robert D'Angelo's place. That place promised to him one sultry evening a lifetime ago, and now offered again only because it was a matter of need, not love.

He crumpled the note that had pulled him back into the painful hell that was his past, letting it drop on a true hero's grave. Walking away, because he wasn't now, as he hadn't been then, worthy of the woman they'd all loved.

Chapter 1

Death hung suspended at arm's length.

She stared with hypnotic horror down the barrel of the gun, seeing no light at the end of that long black tunnel. Only darkness and death.

Hers and her daughter's.

Lifting her gaze from the empty hole that held her demise, she looked into the eyes of her killer. What had she expected to find there? Sympathy? Regret? There was nothing, a flat void of expression as deadly and cold as the bore of the gun.

Was this what her husband had seen, this empty, soulless stare, in the last seconds of his life?

Would this be the last intimacy exchanged between man and wife, this shared precursor to their own end at the same indifferent, yet well-known, hand?

Robert D'Angelo was dead already, his life taken in this same room some months before by this same man. By this man who'd been his friend, his betrayer.

Her heart beat fast and frantically, pounding in her chest, hammering inside her head, the sound amplifying, intensifying like a desperate, unvoiced scream.

Please! I don't want to die!

Tessa sat beside her, calm, fierce, her father's daughter. Instead of begging for mercy, she argued with, even taunted, the man who held their futures in cruel hands. So brave, so confident. So precious. In the twenty-eight years they'd shared, had she told her how precious she was?

An anguished plea burned in her throat, twisting, tearing for release.

Don't take my daughter.

If she jumped forward, if she grabbed the gun, using her body for a shield, perhaps Tessa could get away. There was a chance one of them might survive. Tessa. It should be Tessa, who had so much to live for.

Her breathing caught as an awful realization slammed through her. These could be the last moments of her life.

And then his words, with their terrible finality.

"Sorry, Babs. Nothing personal."

Something moved in his fixed stare. Something so dark and unbelievably terrifying, her plan to save her daughter by sacrificing herself froze in timeless terror.

Pleasure. He was going to enjoy killing them.

An explosion of movement coincided with a shrill of sound. Her dream shattered like that remembered glass as Barbara D'Angelo woke to the ringing of her phone.

It took her a long moment to separate nightmare from reality.

She sat up on the leather love seat, drenched in a sweat of panic. Afternoon sunlight slanted through the windows of the enclosed porch where, after another restless night, she'd fallen, exhausted, to sleep. She forced a constricted breath. Then another. The threat was gone, now behind bars awaiting justice. She was here, safe in her home, not at her husband's office at the mercy of his killer.

The only thing that didn't change upon waking was the fact that her husband was dead.

Vestiges of fear beaded coldly upon her skin. She scrubbed her hands over her face. Only then did she reach for the insistent phone. In another few weeks it would be turned off, the number disconnected as she removed herself forever from this place, from this life. She would be moving on, leaving the past and its ugly scars behind. None too soon.

She lifted the receiver and spoke with what she hoped was coherent civility.

"D'Angelo residence."

An amiable greeting sounded on the other end of the line. It wasn't a solicitor trying to coerce her into opening her checkbook for some worthy cause. It wasn't a friend requesting a long overdue lunch. It wasn't her realtor wondering if the house was ready for the market. It was a voice from the past. One that still echoed, horribly, impossibly, from her nightmare of moments before.

The voice of her husband's murderer.

"Hello, Barbie. Did you think I'd forgotten you?"

For a moment she couldn't respond. Her entire system shriveled into a tiny knot of disbelieving panic. How could it be? How could it be him?

"Babs? You still there? Cat got your tongue?" His chuckle was warm and jovial, making it all the more terrifying. "Nothing to say to me after all we've shared? That's okay. You can just listen. Guess where I am?"

Finally, her shocked stupor ended upon a snap of outrage. "You should be burning in hell, but a life behind bars will have to do."

"I've been to hell, Babs. It was hot and green. But no, I'm not going back there, not for a long while. And right now, there's nothing between me and a fine view of Lake Michigan. Nothing but two lovely young ladies."

He was out. That knowledge stabbed through the protective bubble of her supposed safety, leaving her exposed and alone. She gripped the receiver in sweat-slicked palms, clinging to it in desperate denial. Another more awful notion began to germinate like a toxic virus in her brain. She wanted to hang up, to sever the link, to halt the horrible truth she feared was coming. But she couldn't. She had to know.

"Why are you calling me?" It was little more than a whisper.

"It's a beautiful day. It's great to be alive. At least I'm sure that's what your daughter is thinking. I'm watching her right now."

Barbara's eyes squeezed shut. Panic and helplessness tightened within her chest. Tessa...

"We've been having a wonderful time here on the Navy Pier," Chet Allen continued cheerfully as if he were a part of the outing of school children her daughter was chaperoning in Chicago for the long weekend. "Your Tess particularly enjoyed the display of stained glass inside, but the girls are dragging her down to the Ferris wheel. She's not afraid of heights, is she? I didn't think so. Your scrappy little girl isn't afraid of anything. That's because she doesn't know what you and I know. She doesn't know that her life could be over before she finishes paying for those ice cream cones."

"What do you want?" she all but screamed into the phone.

She could almost see him smiling on the other end of the line, a cold, smug smile of control.

"I want you to do me a favor. But first, a few ground rules just in case you get confused about who's in charge here."

She could hear carnival music in the background and the innocence of happy girlish chatter. She could hardly breathe as she heard him say, "Excuse me, young lady. I think you dropped this."

And then Barbara trembled at the sweetly familiar sound of her adopted grandchild's voice with its delicate Spanish accent.

"Thank you, *señor.*"

Rose. Sweet Rose.

After a brief pause, Chet Allen spoke crisply, clearly, so there would be no mistaking the danger.

"You see how close I am? I could have just as easily

given her a blade between the ribs as returned her bag of cotton candy. Do we understand each other, Barbara? Do you get the picture?"

"Yes," she whispered. She got the picture in Technicolor.

"Good." He was all pleasant humor once again. "Make no mistake. There is nothing, no one, that can come between them and me if you don't do exactly what I tell you. Before you can call your commando son-in-law, before you can scream for help to the Windy City police, I'll have them. They'll be dead. Are we clear on that?"

"Yes." Clear as her Waterford crystal.

"Excellent. Now, back to that favor. You're flying to D.C. this afternoon. I've expressed a ticket to your office. It should be there in about an hour. That doesn't give you much time to pack your party dresses. You've got reservations for two at the Wardman under your maiden name."

"For two?"

"I've arranged for a traveling companion for you, seats 12A and B. Someone who's capable of handling the behind-the-scenes work that needs to be done while you dazzle and distract. The two of you will have a common goal when it comes to saving your daughter's life. Whether you want to tell him why he's got so much at stake is up to you. Just make sure he's motivated to help you. And to help himself."

Surely he couldn't mean…

She couldn't even bring his name into focus for fear of remembering all. She tried to take a breath through the complex emotions wadding in her throat. The effort nearly strangled her. She forced herself to get behind the paralysis of surprise. Not now. Not yet. She could deal with that later. Right now, she had to think of Tessa. She made her mind move forward. Think. "How did you get out?" Suddenly, that mattered, knowing who was pulling the strings. "They said you couldn't make bail. The evidence—"

"Is gone. No more damning paper trail. No more greedy Councilwoman Martinez." She heard his fingers snap. "No more solid case against me. I'm free as a bird with clipped wings. The only ones who can try to put me back in that cage are you and your daughter. But before you get the chance to testify, one of two things will have happened, either you'll join Martinez and disappear or I will."

It took a long moment for her to digest that. What if he was telling the truth? "Martinez…"

"Had an unfortunate accident in her cell. I'd just as soon neither of us have to keep her company. She was really quite unpleasant."

Barbara's mind spun like that dizzying Ferris wheel, trying to make sense of what she was hearing. Martinez was dead. Allen was out on bail. "Who killed her? Why?"

"Let's just say my particular talents were needed to finish up some long overdue business and certain parties were eager to have me on the streets. So I want you to play a game with me. You remember how much I like to play games. This isn't hide-and-seek or spin the bottle. It's a survival game."

"Why should I care if you survive? You killed Robert. You killed my husband."

"That's what I do. And I do it better than anyone else. Don't hold that against me. It was just a job. And now I have another job to do."

"Keeping Tessa and me from going to court," she all but whispered.

Allen laughed off her greatest fear. "Babs, you're not that important in the giant scheme of things. Neither am I. They wouldn't have gotten me out just to tie up my loose ends."

"Who?"

"Them that makes the rules. Rules I have to follow. Rules they've always made me follow even when I didn't want to. It's not about what I want. I can't break those rules. But you can."

"Rules? What are you talking about, Chet?"

"Ask Mac. Those rules used to apply to him, too. He broke them and now they want me to punish him for it. That's my new job, Barbie. That's why I thought you might be interested in playing."

"I don't understand."

The voice on the phone grew harsh and cold as gun metal. "Then let me spell it out for you, Barbara. In fourteen days, I have to appear in court to stand trial for Robert's murder. You and your daughter are the only witnesses who can testify against me. I'm motivated to see that doesn't happen. I have a choice. Either I can silence the both of you or I can disappear. I need help to disappear. In that fourteen days, I have another job to do if I want to live long enough to make that choice, to get that help. I have to silence the only other friend I've ever had. Those are the rules to the game I'm playing. But I'm no fool, Barbie. I know once that job is done, my usefulness will have expired. They may decide not to follow their own rules. Either I'll be buried so far under-cover no one will ever know I existed or I'll be buried next to Robby. I'm not ready for that hot, green hell yet."

"So what do you expect me to do?"

"You don't have to follow rules. You can break them for me. You and Mac. He knows how to play. You have thirteen days to break the rules so Tag doesn't have to die. Then we'll discuss that other choice. The one that involves you and your daughter. You're safe, she's safe for now, as long as you play the game."

"Who makes the rules?"

"Ticktock, Barbie. Better get packing."

"Wait! What is it you want me to do?"

"I'll call you when you get to the Wardman. And Babs, they are lovely girls. You should be proud."

The line went dead.

She sat for long, tense minutes staring at the receiver as if it would yet speak some answer to her. Silence. The only sounds were the tortured gasps of her breathing.

Then, the mellow bongs of the grandfather clock in the living room sounded, tolling out the time and how quickly it was passing. *Ticktock.*

Without thinking, Barbara dialed. A moment passed. Then, at last, a connection.

"Hi, Mom. You should be here to rescue me from

this unruly mob of twelve-year-olds. I'd rather be facing a box of angry jurors."

Tessa's voice, cheerful and alive. Barbara clutched the phone, struggling against a maternal demand that she scream an alarm across the miles that separated them. But Allen was there, watching. She inhaled and let it out in a slow controlled stream before speaking.

"Things going that well. No one said motherhood was a cakewalk."

"It's not for sissies. You could have warned me what I was getting myself into. The other moms have had a dozen years to get used to the idea and I've only had a few months. But you know what? I wouldn't have missed this for the world."

Emotion thickened in Barbara's throat as she pictured her toughly independent daughter overwrought by the pleasures of parenting. Pleasures that had slipped quietly and almost unnoticed away from the two of them during Tessa's growing-up years. She blinked back the burn of tears as she phrased her words, knowing someone was nearby, watching Tessa's reactions to whatever she said. "Enjoy yourself, but be careful. Chicago can be a dangerous place. You need to be ready to protect those little girls against anything. And yourself, too."

"Are you suggesting I should have packed my piece to go on a school field trip?" She laughed. Then the ever practical side of her personality took over. "Don't worry, Mom. Jack trusted me to make sure nothing ever happens to Rose and I take that very seriously. I'd never let him down."

"I love you, Tessa."

The impulsive statement was met with the silence of surprise. There was still too much healing to do between them for Barbara to have expected a reply. So instead, she filled the uncomfortable void with light-hearted small talk. It wouldn't do for Tessa to guess the truth about the danger she was in. Not when she was vulnerable, unprepared and unarmed and caring for a group of children. Because Barbara knew her daughter, knew she would rush headlong into a con-frontation that could cost her her life and the life of the child she loved. Those were the risks she, herself, would take to keep them safe and unsuspecting.

"Tell Rose I said hello and not to eat too much junk food."

"Ha! You tell her. Twelve-year-olds think sugar is a primary food group. How are things holding together at the office?"

"Fine," she lied. "Everything's under control here. You just concentrate on having a good time."

"On keeping my sanity, you mean. Gotta go. See ya later this week."

Sitting there, listening to dead air as her inner spirit wept, Barbara made a promise to do anything neces-sary to see her daughter safely home.

Even if that meant making a deal with a devil.

"Are you sure you can handle everything until Jack gets back?"

From the front-row seat of his wheelchair, Michael Chaney watched his son's mother-in-law pace the length of the office as if it were a fashion runway. She was the most sophisticated creature the ex-cop had ever known. All class, all the time. Not intentional, just instinctual. That classiness had been passed down to the woman his son married, along with a not-so-delicate grit. Despite the polish, despite the poise, that sandpapery grit was showing on Barbara D'Angelo like the ragged edge of a crooked slip hanging below her stylish hemline. Something was wrong. Something that had to do with the suitcase and matching overnight bag she dragged into the office behind her. Something to do with the airline ticket she held clenched in one white-knuckled hand. But because he was an ex-cop, as well as her friend, he approached the situation carefully.

Michael snorted at her question. "I've handled worse than eight badass bodyguards-in-training. Stan's working with them this week, probably beating them over the head with his cane to keep their attention focused on surveillance equipment instead of that hot little pilot with her long, long legs."

That won a rueful smile. "Sounds like you've been doing some surveillance yourself."

"I'm crippled, not dead. I'll handle the phones and the interviews, and Stan will keep the probbies in line. Hey, no worries."

But he could sense worries aplenty behind her artfully made-up surface. Barbara knew it. And she couldn't afford to rouse his suspicions.

He'd know if she made one tiny slip. Family was the only thing that would wear concern into her flawless face. Nothing was wrong there that he knew of and she had to see that he continued to believe that. As far as he knew, Barbara was loving her stint behind the desk of Personal Protection Professionals. Who would have guessed? Less than a year ago, she'd been a regular on the society page, hosting elaborate fundraisers for charities and her husband's political aspirations. Her biggest worries then had been whether the hired kitchen staff could keep up with the demand for shrimp puffs. Then a gunshot ended that superficial existence.

All Michael Chaney knew, from what she'd told him, was that at fifty, she was a widow whose résumé was as trophy wife. She had no skills, no passions, no purpose. Her sons lived on different sides of the country and her daughter might as well live on another planet for the distance that separated them. She was alone for the first time in her life, though she'd been lonely for years. Hard to believe, but she'd made him into a believer.

And then Jack Chaney proposed marriage to her daughter and a business arrangement to her.

She'd been surprised, doubtful and, more than that, genuinely excited. A job opportunity. A chance to be a part of something real and important and growing, like her relationship with her daughter now that the secrets between them had been torn wide open. Office manager for Personal Protection Professionals, or Lone Wolf's Warriors, as Tessa liked to call it after Jack's former black ops code name. They'd rented space in the center of a run-down strip mall, wedged between the hot pink vertical blinds of a hair salon and the flickering neons of an income tax service. The sign was still so new the paint looked wet. Her job was to coordinate between the training compound that housed Jack and his family, and the office; paying bills and spearheading the background checks with the elder Chaney and Stan Kovacs, his partner from their days on the streets before a criminal's bullet put Michael in a wheelchair. And though this was the first paycheck-earning job she'd ever had, Barbara took it seriously. She wouldn't let Jack's unsubstantiated faith in her down for anything.

And one of the things she's promised him was to take care of his new wife and their adopted daughter when he was away. And she wouldn't break that promise.

Barbara finally gave up her aggressive travels and collapsed gracefully into a utilitarian office chair. She looked like a Saks Fifth Avenue marionette with the strings abruptly severed; inside, her emotions were just as tangled. "Where is Jack, anyway?"

"Someplace in Mexico doing a favor for his buddy Russell. He's not very good at cards and letters when he's in the field, but he'll check in when he's supposed to. Anything you want me to tell him?"

There it was. The opening Barbara had waited for. The chance to unload the tension and terror continuing to build behind her composed facade. But she kept it to herself, hugged it close, as tight as she would have held to those two unsuspecting girls had they stepped into the office at this moment. Because she knew what Chet Allen was and what he was capable of doing. She forced a smile. If Jack had been here, if she was able to get hold of him, he'd know just what to do. He knew the kind of man Allen was, too, and he'd know how to handle this dangerous situation. But Jack wasn't here and she couldn't ask his advice. So she'd have to trust her own instincts. And pray she was doing the right thing.

"Tell him Tessa and Rose send their love. And that I'm taking care of things."

"What things, Barbara? What things are you taking care of?"

There was no escaping that blunt question. She stared down at the ticket crushed in her hand. A ticket leading toward troubles untold and a madman on the loose. And, apparently, a long overdue reunion. The significance was too enormous to consider on top of all else.

But one thing she did know. If Allen was following her to D.C., he wouldn't be here threatening her family. That, alone, was worth the risk she was taking.

And then there was that other matter Allen had hinted at. The matter she'd squeezed out of her thoughts but had her heart beating a rapid tempo of anticipation.

Taggert McGee.

"Things I should have dealt with a long, long time ago," was the answer that would have to satisfy him. The honk of her cab's horn relieved her from further awkward evasion. She took a shaky breath and regarded Michael Chaney through misting eyes. "Behave. I'll be back…in a few days."

But would she be returning to the life she was learning to love and the new family she couldn't live without?

That, she realized as she towed her luggage out the door, was now in her hands. Hands that were damp and trembling.

"Excuse me. Has the passenger in seat 12B checked in yet?"

The airline attendant who'd just given the last call for her flight regarded Barbara with a regretful smile. "I'm sorry, ma'am. Not that I'm aware of. You'll have to board now."

She scanned the empty rows of form-fitted seats in the gate area as if she'd find her traveling companion still there like an unattended bag. Panic twisted beneath her ribs. "Are you sure?"

The attendant's smile never wavered. "Yes, ma'am. You'll have to board now. There's another flight if your friend arrives too late."

Too late.

Too late for whom? For the daughter and grandchild at the mercy of a maniac? A deadly lunatic, government-trained to do only one thing and do it well. A man like that didn't value life. Not even his own. And that made him the worst kind of threat.

She was right to be afraid.

The moment she recognized his voice on her home phone, Barbara had shifted into a numb sort of overdrive. She'd called no one after confirming Tessa's safety. A tenuous condition. Whether she remained in that state of grace was up to Barbara, and that burden weighed like a Mack truck parked atop her heart. What could she do but follow Allen's dictates? Who could she call for help? The police were no match for a man like Chet. Not after Robert's murder and not now. Even after she, Tessa and Jack had snared him and the councilwoman he'd worked for, the justice system had somehow opened their doors to put him back into a society where he didn't belong. If she reached out to the world around her for assistance, he would know. Somehow, he would know. And the consequences were too awful to consider.

So she'd locked the doors of her palatial home and driven off in her big luxury car. She went to the office of Personal Protection Professionals, where currently she was the entire office staff. And with all that expertise, all that well-honed skill surrounding her, available upon her single word, she hadn't dared speak it.

If she did, somehow he would know. And the two she loved most in the world would die.

There were only two people who'd ever been able to handle Chet Allen. One, her husband, was dead. The other belonged to the unclaimed seat.

"Please, ma'am." The attendant gestured down the tunnel where the sound of her jet whined impatiently.

Lifting her carry-on, Barbara gave the terminal hall one last glance, then committed to the rush down the gangway. A relieved attendant directed her to her seat in the full main cabin. Two empty seats together. Too late now to regret her decision to comply with Chet Allen's plan. She'd just have to find a way to handle things in Washington on her own. Whatever those things might be.

The overhead compartment was already full. While

those seated around her glared at the delay, Barbara wrestled with her bag, trying to force it into the narrow space remaining. The Fasten Seat Belts tone sounded twice, urging her to hurry. Frustration knotted in her throat and burned behind her eyes. Just as the need to weep nearly overpowered, a man reached up to clear the necessary space into which her bag fit snugly.

"Thank you."

Taking a jerking breath, she looked over her shoulder to her rescuer, but any other words died on her lips. Her pathetically grateful smile froze there.

"Hello, Barbara."

She couldn't draw a breath. Her head grew light, her vision unreliable. But there was no confusing the man in the aisle beside her with any other.

How could one forget the man who had fathered a child and then left her and the baby for another man to raise as his own? The man she must now depend upon to save that precious child's life.

Chapter 2

He'd stood behind the forest of racks at the gift shop for almost fifteen minutes staring, not at the line of passengers being herded onto the plane, but at the tattered papers in his hand. A sensational newspaper clipping, an airline ticket and a short note from a one-time friend he'd never expected to hear from again. But it wasn't the sordid nature of the article dealing with a six-month-old murder case, or the tersely worded invitation that brought him to this place. It was one fact. That fact had beaten like a wild, hopeful heart every mile of the hard day's drive to get to Detroit Metro.

Barbara Calvin D'Angelo was free again.

Just seeing her name in the article ripped into him

with all the delicacy of a chest cutter, exposing emotions still raw and pulsing with desperate life. The years didn't matter. He'd last seen her, last touched her, last heard her soft voice more than three decades ago, but the memories were as fresh as the strong aroma of coffee in a vacuum-packed jar. Tear back the protective cover and the immediacy of feelings long stored away overwhelmed him.

A fool's errand. That's what he was on.

He'd told himself that at every mile marker, too. But it was Barbara who drew him like a beacon. The memory of her was a light so bright it burned into the brain. Yet, he couldn't look away, despite the pain. Remembering her throbbed with toothache intensity clear to his soul, an insistence that may have dulled but never quite went away. It was all he could do not to moan that anguish aloud. Instead, it wailed through his spirit, a mournful banshee of regret and loss. Chased with a sharp edge of anticipation.

Finally, he had his excuse. His reason for seeking out that one wonderful spark from his past that had kept him alive. And he couldn't pass it up.

A smart man would have left well enough alone. He would have crumpled up the unwelcome news and used it to flame the evening's fire. But the spark had taken hold. And once it began to burn, it would not be contained or denied.

He had to see her again. If for no other reason than to put the memories to rest.

He knew time had preserved and sugarcoated his treasured recollections. He remembered the sweetness of those moments with a heart-piercing pleasure so pure, so right, he knew they couldn't be real. The passing of years and the bitter roads he'd traveled only made them seem perfect. Still, he couldn't let them go. Barbara had been the one good thing he looked back upon, the one slice of recall he didn't doubt was real. He shouldn't risk tarnishing that by opening those memories to the harshness that had transpired between that fragile then and this bleak now. He'd be snuffing out his one faint flicker of contentment.

Maybe that's why he was here. To grind out that relentless ember beneath his heel so he could move on.

Move on to what?

The only direction he'd ever wanted to take was the one Barbara D'Angelo was heading. She was his North Star and home was wherever she resided.

Sheer foolishness, of course. But the poet's soul that used to dwell inside him was as hard to crush as that poignant flame of hope.

Last chance. Last chance to just walk away and head north, preserving his memories in vacuum-sealed museum quality and his emotions in their static state. The first he could continue to take out, to dust off and admire with a dreamy wistfulness, and the other he could simply continue to endure. But if he stayed and made Barbara D'Angelo's business his own, all that would drastically alter.

Go. Don't be a fool. Nothing has changed.

But then that poet's heart and a fool's footsteps carried him onto the plane and back into her life.

She said something. He couldn't hear the words

over the sudden loud humming in his head that rivaled the drone of the turbine engines. The surroundings faded out into soft focus until only she existed in a sharp field of vision.

She hadn't changed at all.

She was still slender, stylishly dressed in charcoal-gray slacks and a two-piece sweater of sparkly silver thread. Blond hair framed her face in a youthful cut that just brushed her shoulders. And that face...mind-stunningly beautiful. A face that launched a thousand dreams, though none of them came true.

But of course, when she turned toward him, standing so close he could hear her sudden inhalation, he noticed the patina of age that settled over her with grace and protective care. Her eyes were a soft gray, malleable yet enduring like pewter. Her mouth was all sweet curves and wistful angles. High cheekbones and a delicate jaw lent her a classic loveliness, but all those attributes that made her gorgeous didn't make her glow. That came from the inner beauty of Barbara D'Angelo. Her goodness shone through, transforming mere breathtaking to an ethereal perfection.

Those gray eyes widened. Those tender lips parted in shock. She didn't move. He didn't think she even breathed.

"Hello, Barbara."

It took her a moment to say his name. She looked so startled, he doubted she remembered her own. Then she said it in a quavery whisper and his heart rolled over.

"Hello, Tag."

Her surprise bled away into a palette of emotions,

all of them as bittersweet as the moment. Delight, guilt, relief, remembrance, and finally, pain. Each dawned with stunning intensity, like a spectacular new sunrise or sunset. He stood and simply marveled.

How had he ever thought he could confront the past with a stoic demeanor? He was shaking inside like a schoolboy. She still had that effect on him. Reducing him, while at the same time making him want to be more.

Get a grip, man.

Thirty years had passed. This was not the same girl who'd sent him off to war with promises she couldn't keep. This woman had been another man's wife, the mother to his children. And he was suddenly, brutally, aware that he couldn't reverse time, that he couldn't return them to that golden slice of innocence where she would rush into his arms and return to him his happily-ever-after dream. That dream had died when Robert D'Angelo returned from leave wearing a grin and a wedding ring.

He'd been a fool to come. What had he been thinking?

His jaw tightened. Disillusionment lent a saving detachment to his outward appearance. Get tough, get through it and get out alive. His motto from Southeast Asia still served him in a crisis. He'd survived worse. He'd survive this moment with grace under fire and escape before his heart was a repeat casualty.

"I didn't think… I wasn't sure… I mean, I didn't know if you'd—" She broke off the uncharacteristic stammer to demand, "What are you doing here? Why did you come?"

He read shades of meaning in her bewildered questions. *After all these years. After abandoning our friendship. After no word for so long.* Then her gaze toughened to, *How dare you just show up now?* Her confrontational glare helped him reinforce a wary stance.

"I heard about Robert."

Anguish cut across her stare, crushing the momentary rebellion. Her right hand moved to cover her left, where she still wore a ring. She wet her lips, the gesture achingly vulnerable. Then the edge was back, a tight, honed look he'd never seen from her before.

But then a lot had happened since the last time they were together.

"That was over six months ago." The accusation was unmistakable.

"I've been kind of isolated."

"For the last thirty years?" Her gaze narrowed into an impressive demand for atonement. One he couldn't make.

One he shouldn't have to make. One he sure as hell couldn't tell her about. Even if he knew. His own gaze chilled.

"You might say that."

His mild answer wasn't what she wanted to hear. Her response crackled with raw feeling.

"It was a nice funeral. You should have been there."

"I would have been there, had I known. For Robert. For you." That last was said more softly than he'd intended.

Anger and hurt built like thunderheads. Her glacial stare flashed lightning. Her voice rumbled thunder.

"Thank you for the sentiment. I'll let my family know that my husband's best friend who fell off the face of the earth for thirty years sends his condolences. And in person, at that."

"Your friend, too, Barbara."

"My friend," she mused as if trying to fit that concept together with the disparity of his absence.

"I'm—"

"Sorry?" Her voice notched up an octave. "Don't you dare say you're sorry. Not about anything. You don't have the right to be sorry."

"I was going to say I'm here now. Or would you rather I not be?" His cool tone had her reining in her anger.

"Yes…no." Clearly flustered, she stabbed her fingers back through her baby-fine hair and then fisted them. "I don't know. It's so…unexpected you being here. I don't know what to think or feel."

"I didn't mean to crowd you, Barb. Maybe I should go."

"No."

She took an involuntary step forward, her expression sharp with alarm.

"Please take your seats," the stewardess urged with a smiling forcefulness.

Without another word, Barbara abandoned her aggressive stance to slide into the window seat and fasten her seat belt. McGee settled beside her and did likewise. But what held them tighter, more constrictively, were the questions, the confusion over why they'd been brought back together.

Chet Allen.

Chet had arranged this meeting. Barbara fought back a surge of renewed despair. He'd brought Taggert McGee back into her life. Why? After so many years, why now? Why now, when she was just starting to get a new routine on track, would he derail it so abruptly with this ghost from her past? What kind of sadistic revenge was he manipulating her into, first by threatening her daughter and granddaughter and now by forcing her to deal with what she'd been trying to deny?

The fact was that Tag McGee was her daughter's father, and despite the pain, the betrayal, the emptiness of loss, she'd never loved another the way she had loved him. Perhaps Chet had no idea what he was stirring up with his cryptic invitations.

Or perhaps he did.

Chet's motives would have to wait. For the moment, it took all her energy just to maintain a shred of composure.

They began to taxi toward an unplanned destination, toward a purpose unknown to her. Much like this awkward and emotionally explosive meeting. She sat stiffly as the plane left the ground, staring out the window with a concentrated lack of focus as the plane parted the clouds in a climb toward cruising altitude. If only her thoughts would level out as easily.

Taggert McGee. The unexpected blast from her past Chet alluded to sent her heart for a loop.

She had imagined what she'd say to him if they ever met again. She'd imagined it a thousand times over the course of thirty years, even as the unlikelihood of that happening dimmed with the passage of time. She'd dreamed of the cathartic things she'd hurl at him, words of hurt and blame and retribution, demanding an accounting for his actions when no excuse, no reason could come close to justifying the agony he'd put her through. She'd planned the moment—what she'd wear, how she'd toss her head with indignant disdain, how she'd reduce him to shamed attrition. Her chance had come and gone with a whimper instead of a roar.

And now she had to decide how to treat this return of the prodigal lover under less than ideal circumstances. The scripted meeting was unfolding without a hitch, but it wasn't at her direction. This time, she had more at stake than bruised pride and shattered dreams. Lives were at stake, if a madman's words could be believed. That was just the wake-up slap back to reality she needed to look at Taggert McGee and really see him as he was, instead of through the eyes of a needy teenager.

He wasn't that lean, wiry boy surrounded by shyness and a natural, easy grace. He wasn't the all-star running back or the all-city catcher who dreamed of going to college on a sports scholarship. He wasn't the boy with the engaging gentleness to his manner that belied his aggressive pursuits of sports, hunting and boxing. He wasn't the same person who wooed her with his love of poetry and solitude rather than the acid rock and radical causes of the era. This wasn't the Taggert McGee who, at eighteen, had stood with duffel bag in hand, his fair hair buzzed down to the scalp, his handsome features gaunt, his mild, deep-set blue eyes fierce with turmoil as the bus pulled in behind him. She hadn't known then that that emotional image would have to last her for more than thirty years.

He'd been eighteen, her first love, and he'd broken her heart like none before or after.

This was no boy going off to war come to say his last farewells. This specter from the past, wearing loose cargo jeans and a battered brown leather bomber jacket over plaid flannel, had none of that lost look of innocence. He was all contained authority, intense confidence and unapologetic masculinity with his thinning hair and ice-blue, vise-grip gaze that told her nothing. He'd aged well, like Scotch whiskey, acquiring a mellow depth and complexity she found confusingly enticing. And beneath the controlled veneer, the casual attire, the nonthreatening receding hairline, he positively sparked with an electrifying sex appeal.

Or was that just her hormones inappropriately indulging in one last riotous adrenaline-induced hurrah?

What frustrated her, what made her testy, was his total imperviousness to his effect on her.

"Can I get you something to drink?"

She glanced up, surprised to see the beverage cart in the aisle. "Coffee, please." With a chaser of that fine Scotch would be nice.

She started to reach for her cup, then balked when Tag reached for it at the same time. She eased back to let him perform the perfunctory courtesy of passing the hot coffee over to her.

Lord, he smelled delicious. Like cedar chips and

spruce boughs. She forced herself not to inhale, to look straight ahead as she sipped the welcome heat that burned and calmed all at the same time.

For heaven's sake, she was no kid to be swept away by a sinewy smile and great bone structure. She'd been married to the same man for more than thirty years, had borne three children and was a grandmother.

And even if she was feeling suddenly as randy as a debutante, she wouldn't choose this man to indulge her late-life passions with. He was poison to her system, a danger to her emotional health. It took her thirty years to recover from the unsettling lurch in which he'd left her. She wouldn't risk that loss of equilibrium again.

And next tò her, Tag was thinking much the same thing.

Get a grip, McGee. She's not that little pep-club president anymore. She's a woman who's known her share of love and loss, and she's definitely written you off in the latter category.

He'd sit back and enjoy the ride. He'd listen to Chet's spiel, whatever it might be, thank him, but no thanks, wish Barbara well and be on his way by nightfall. He didn't know what Chet was up to and didn't want to find out. With the twisted way his friend's mind worked, it could be anything from a simple reunion to a plunge into deadly intrigue. And he wanted no part of it. Not anymore. And not with Barbara at his side. He had the return ticket in his jacket. He could get as far as the bridge before exhaustion claimed him. He could disappear back into that safety zone of anonymity he'd made for himself. And maybe he'd sleep without dreams.

There was nothing for him here. Like the old saying went, he couldn't go home again.

And he definitely couldn't imagine going home to the palace where Barbara and Robert D'Angelo had lived.

He took the envelope from Chet Allen out of his coat pocket and carefully unfolded it so he could remove the single clipping. It was a sparse teaser of a story concerning the suspected suicide of a popular district attorney that turned out to be murder. A complex scheme of drug trafficking involving the equally high visibility of a councilwoman running for the same political seat. The story to follow on page three had not been included. Purposefully, Tag assumed, to pique his curiosity and bring him here, to these economy class seats.

The photo accompanying the story was of Robert and Barbara meeting and greeting in front of their home. Grimly, Tag assessed the outward trappings of the life Barbara had led. The stately elegance of the Tudor suited her. He could imagine her socializing at the door with her genuine smile and gracious manner. He could picture Rob beside her, everyone's favorite host. The perfect couple living the all-American dream.

So why was Rob D'Angelo dead and Barbara here beside him?

He never would have believed suicide. Robert D'Angelo was the most focused and determined individual he'd ever known. Upper middle class striving for millionaire and all the perks that went with it. That was Rob. He'd always known exactly what he wanted and he got it all, everything...and everyone. He'd been a top student, a model citizen, a good friend, and Tag didn't begrudge him any of it, not even Barbara. He was the one fathers wanted their daughters to date, the one people were eager to trust, the one most likely to succeed. But he hadn't gotten to keep his fame and fortune for long.

"Who killed him?"

Barbara didn't seem surprised by the sudden question. She apparently had been waiting for it, preparing for it, if her deadpan answer was any indication.

"Chet Allen."

Tag couldn't have been more shocked if she'd named the pope as the perpetrator.

"Chet? Chet killed Rob?" His mind couldn't contain that knowledge. There had to be some mistake.

The three of them, the Three Musketeers Barbara had called them. All so different, yet held so tightly together by bonds of friendship since grade school. Since before social status mattered. He could envision them together on any number of teen escapades, from scoring illegal alcohol for a party to harmless pranks conceived by Rob and executed to perfection by Chet. The planner, the doer and the dreamer. That had been the three of them. The three of them, all in love with the same girl.

"I don't believe it."

"Believe it. Your friend Allen is one sick, dangerous

man. Robert underestimated him and now he's dead. He would have gotten away with it, too, except for one thing. He underestimated my daughter. And her new husband. They caught him and they brought him to justice, but justice let them down."

"He walked."

"Like a ghost. Or at least, that's what he plans. You don't sound surprised."

"Let me guess who did the paperwork with a federal seal of approval."

They both were silent for a moment, sharing their unspoken opinion of the various agencies that had employed Allen. And McGee.

"Where is he now?"

"Not as far away as I'd hoped he'd be. You know Chet. You know how he thinks, how he reacts."

She glanced at him and then away, the gesture furtive, compelling. Needy. Expectant. His instincts quivered on alert. His tone grew as thin and deadly as a trip wire.

"And you want me to do what, exactly? Catch him? Kill him? I don't do that kind of thing anymore."

"It's not about what I want. It's Chet. It's the game he's playing." She looked back at Tag then, her stare direct and intense. "How did he get you here?"

Tag squirmed inwardly but kept his reply curt and concise. "He sent this clipping, and he said you needed me."

That was all. Barbara needed him. And it would have brought him back from hell without the necessity of explanation.

"So," he continued, "here I am. What do you need me to do?"

For all the turmoil and terror within her heart and mind, Barbara's answer was amazingly calm.

"Chet Allen has threatened my daughter and her child unless I do exactly as he tells me. A sort of demented Simon Says. I want you to help me keep them alive. That's my agenda. I don't know what Chet has planned. All I know is I'm willing to play along if it means keeping them safe."

She paused, then added the twist Chet had provided for his amusement.

"And he wants you to play the game with me."

Chapter 3

He listened as she filled him in on most of what Chet had told her, leaving out only one thing. The danger to him. She couldn't afford to spook him, not with all she had at stake. She wouldn't have doubted the Tag she'd known. But that was a long time ago, and he'd let her down then. So why would she risk so much in hopes that his tenuous integrity remained? She didn't want him to run, and she didn't want to be alone. So she omitted that one important fact. Trying to excuse the gnawing guilt that grew each time she avoided the opportunity to tell him.

She wouldn't consider his life in the balance. She would only think of Tessa and Rose. And of herself. As Tag McGee had thought only of himself.

He sat still and attentive, absorbing and assimilating like a good soldier, the way Robert had after he'd come back to discuss their future, emotionlessly, expressionlessly. As if he were being briefed for combat. But wasn't that really the case? Wasn't she preparing him to confront Allen upon the battlefield his twisted brain had created?

As she laid out the reasons for her willingness to be Chet's pawn, to take the risk that Allen's game wouldn't end with her demise, she waited to see a flicker of that same parental concern in Tag's unwavering stare. And was disappointed.

If he felt any panic over the fate of their child, if he experienced any sympathy for the emotions crushing within her, he kept them isolated behind an expression so stoic it tore through her heart. Didn't he care that his daughter was in danger? Didn't the thought of their peril touch upon any fond chord in his memory?

Apparently not.

But she didn't need Tag McGee to console her. She didn't need his platitudes and professions of concern. Not after all this time. What she needed from him was what she saw. A close-lipped stranger. A tough-minded former marine. A hero who would step in to eliminate the threat Chet Allen brought into their lives. And she'd be a fool to expect anything more.

She finished the briefing and took a stabilizing breath.

"So, what do you think it means?"

It took him a moment to respond to her question with one of his own.

"What does what mean?"

"Them that makes the rules. That's what Chet said. Who are they? What is he talking about? What does he want from us?"

His answer crippled her confidence.

"I have no idea."

Perhaps he felt some slight regret when her features fell in despair for he was quick to continue.

"I haven't seen or heard from Chet since I left the service. I don't know what he's been involved in. I wouldn't have thought him capable of this." He lifted the clipping, then crumpled it in one savage spasm of his hand. "I don't have any answers, Barbara. Only questions, just like you. I guess we'll just have to see what Chet has in mind when we get to D.C."

He was going to help her.

Relief shivered along her limbs, weakening the paralysis of fear. McGee was going to help them.

He looked away from the blatant gratitude in her gaze and partially stood to slip out of his jacket. He folded it and then draped the worn leather along the armrest between them, creating a symbolic barrier. Then, he settled into his seat and closed his eyes, building a stockade against further conversation, as well.

Barbara's disillusionment escaped on a soft breath.

So much for their reunion.

Apparently he had no questions regarding her life over the past thirty years, no desire to catch up on what occurred between the time that bus had pulled out, leaving a young girl alone, and now, when his shuttered mood left the woman she'd become feeling just

as isolated. He hadn't even asked to see a picture of
Tessa. Which meant he had no interest. Fine. No
problem. If he didn't want to bring up that mutual
piece of their past, neither would she. He'd made no
effort to make Tessa part of his life and she wouldn't
push it now. Barbara swallowed down the huge knot
of hope that had built inside her and let angry disappointment burn in its place. She could put her head and
heart on hold. After all, it was the one skill she'd per-
fected over those long, lonely years.

As she squirmed in her seat to find a comfortable
position, her elbow nudged his coat. It slid toward her
and as she pushed it back into its previous position, a
narrow folder slipped from an inside pocket to land at
her feet. She recognized the ticket portfolio as she
bent to pick it up. Seat 12B. And beneath it, another
card. One glance told her everything.

A return dated for this evening.

Her insides froze at the significance. His quick exit
plan was already in motion.

She was on her own.

The notion that she'd be able to find sleep in her
economy class seat never occurred to Barbara. Too
many things swirled through her mind. Things too
horrible to bring into focus, like her daughter's safety.
Things too tenuous to wish for, like Tag's continued
support. She'd meant only to close her eyes for an
instant to relieve the ache building behind them and
seemingly in the next second, she heard the pilot's
droning voice announcing their arrival.

Surprised and almost guilty, she straightened in her seat. The subtle squaring motion beside her hinted that McGee had been watching her sleep. An odd, discomforting quiver went through her. She wasn't sure she liked the idea of him observing her in such a relaxed and vulnerable state. Vulnerable was the last impression she wanted him to have of her. Six months ago, yes, it would be true. If not vulnerable, then simply naive in her own security. Burying a husband and staring down the barrel of a gun had gone a long way toward changing that blissful existence.

She couldn't afford to let her guard down for an instant. Not with Chet Allen casting a cold shadow over her. Not with Taggert McGee refusing to commit to her cause.

Toughness wasn't something inbred in her. She'd been raised a hothouse flower, dependent upon exacting care, not as a self-sufficient cactus, using spines and self-deprivation as a means to survive. Her daughter was like that. And so, apparently, was the father Tessa had never met. It was either grow and thrive where you're planted, or wither up and die. Until now, Barbara hadn't considered herself as the prickly type. But she would learn. She would learn if it meant keeping her daughter and granddaughter alive. If, to be totally honest with herself, it meant keeping the man beside her from Allen's crosshairs.

Fortified by rest and by the image of her new thorny self, Barbara released her seat belt at the flight attendant's prompting and waited for Tag to step out into the aisle so she could retrieve her bag. They stood together like strangers who happened to travel on the same plane, ignoring each other until the line began to move slowly toward the exit. As they started forward, the light touch of Tag's hand on her elbow had her looking back at him. Dark glasses hid his gaze. His attention moved about the cabin as he spoke with a quiet intensity.

"Go to the Wardman. I'll meet you there."

Her alarm must have telegraphed in her expression for he was quick to reassure her.

"Check in and I'll meet you in the room. For now, I think it's best if we're not seen together."

Best for whom? Why the secrecy? But her demand would have to wait as they were jostled ahead down the narrow aisle. By the time she had elbow room on the gangway, Tag was no longer behind her. A quick glance revealed him near the cabin door where he'd stepped aside to let others go before him. Putting distance between them.

Shouldering her carry-on, Barbara turned and strode purposefully into the terminal. She refused to think of it as being abandoned all over again as she claimed her luggage and hailed a cab. As the busy network of highways carried her toward the outskirts of the nation's capital, she blocked everything from her mind except the sound of Rose's innocent laughter on the phone. An ache gathered in her soul. How she loved that little girl who had been all too briefly in her life. How she loved the daughter who only recently would allow her to show it. Nothing else mattered. Not her personal jeopardy. Not her uneasy alliance with a ghost from her past.

The cab climbed up the flower-lined residential streets toward the stately hotel. She'd stayed at the Wardman a long time ago, when she'd come to meet her returning war hero husband on the eve of his receipt of his Purple Heart. Robert had insisted she leave the then three-year-old Tessa behind with her parents, claiming this would be the honeymoon they'd never had. They had no practice at playing man and wife, just hasty vows said in a judge's chambers before he returned to his unit to be shipped overseas. They'd never even been intimate. Just some hasty groping at a drive-in before she'd fallen head over heart for his best friend and a quick kiss at the judge's urging. He'd been looking forward to this reunion for three long years, he'd told her. Just as she'd been dreading it.

Not much had changed, she thought, entering the lobby. Only the man involved. Another stranger whom fate had thrust into her life to irrevocably change it. Not this time. This time, she'd remain in control of her own destiny rather than place it in the sometimes crushing, sometimes uncaring grip of another. She'd learned that lesson, too.

"The room's already been prepaid, Ms. Calvin," the chipper desk clerk advised as she reached for her purse. "Enjoy your stay."

She smiled. Not likely. Not with Tag hoarding secrets and Chet indulging in games. Not when she was checking into a hotel under a fake identity for purposes unknown. If it was covert playtime between the two men, she resented having to play along. But she would; she had to, for now.

She followed the bellhop, not to the elevators for the highrise conference tower but down a glassed hall to the older portion of the hotel. He accepted her tip with another optimistic wish that she enjoy herself before she closed the door to the room, shutting off the need to pretend that she was just another guest in D.C. there to partake of the energetic nightlife and tourist sights. Throwing the dead bolt, she let her rigid shoulders relax a notch. Okay, first step completed. I'm here, Chet. Now what?

"He left flowers and an envelope on the table by the window."

The sudden intrusion of a man's voice had her nearly clearing the hug of her Italian leather shoes as Tag McGee stepped from the dressing area. She didn't bother to ask how he'd gotten in the room. She was too busy trying to get her heartbeat under control.

"I haven't opened it yet," he continued. "Shall we see what he has to say?"

"As long as it's not, 'Have a nice stay.'"

Barbara waved off the questioning look and focused on the antique drop leaf positioned decoratively in front of the privacy sheers. A beautiful arrangement of spring flowers in shades of pink and blue was displayed in a crystal vase. With a chill of recall, she remembered a similar spray at her husband's funeral because it was the only one that had come with no card.

Had those come from Chet, as well?

Regarding the blooms with a frown, Barbara reached for the plain envelope propped up against the vase. It contained a single typewritten sheet.

"Mac and Barbie. My two favorite people together again. You have reservations on the twilight monument tour. Don't be late."

Tag didn't respond to her flat reading of the note. His expression was uncommunicative. And suddenly she was furious. At his indifference. At her own drowning sense of being in over her head. Barbara returned the paper to the envelope, the burn of betrayal rising in a bitter tide. Her words were tainted by the acidic taste.

"Too bad you'll miss it, McGee. You won't have enough time to catch your flight."

He didn't react with what would have been a satisfying degree of guilt or shame. If he wondered how she'd gotten that bit of information, he didn't express it. His response was a continued unflappable cool. "I'll get another one. Chet wants us both to play follow the leader with him, for whatever reason, so I guess I'll play along. For now."

Not exactly the reassurance she'd hoped for, but it was enough. She wasn't facing Allen alone, at least not yet.

To cover her relief and her uneasiness with McGee, she made a show of checking over their accommodations. It was a large, impressive room designed with a comfortable dignity and filled with originals, from the furniture to the art and knickknacks. Foremost, of course, was the dominating king-size bed. The sight of Tag's duffel bag upon the jacquard coverlet made her feel like that awkward honeymooner all over again. And suddenly the room wasn't large enough.

"The monument tour," she mused to hide her nervousness. "Do you think he'll try to contact us then?"

"Maybe," was Tag's noncommittal reply.

"Why Washington? Why couldn't he just tell us what was going on without all this cloak-and-dagger nonsense?" Her tone grew testy with frustration and an undercurrent of fear. She had no talent for cloak-and-dagger games. That was McGee's area, his and Allen's. So why include her in the play? Her cheerleading days had passed a long, long time ago. Why pull her in from the spectating sidelines now?

"Because them that makes the rules are here."

His quiet summation caught her off guard and had her swiveling to level a demanding stare. "I thought you said you didn't know what he meant by that or who they were?"

"I said I didn't know what he meant by it." That's all he would volunteer.

He stood there, so maddeningly inscrutable, the man who'd evolved from the boy she'd known and loved. The boy who had abandoned his obligations to her and the child they'd made between them. A stranger to her now. Spare of frame and expression. Making her walk a tightrope of emotions while he was firm-footed on the ground. What did she owe him? What reason could she name to put his welfare above those she cared for? Then she heard herself speak.

"They're the ones who want you dead."

He never even blinked. Perhaps he hadn't understood her.

So she elaborated.

"They're the ones who want Chet to kill you."

Then came his jaw-dropping answer.

"I know."

"You know?"

"I figured as much when I got the note from Chet. He used you to draw me out."

"You knew that. You knew that and still you came?" She couldn't get her thoughts around the magnitude of that. "Why? Why would you walk right into what could be a trap?"

"It was bound to happen sooner or later. Just a matter of time." His brief hesitation before speaking that bland explanation told her it wasn't the entire truth.

Because of her? Was that why? She crushed that fleeting wish. After not contacting her for thirty years, he was willing to walk into a bullet for her now? Then his even softer question threw everything else out the window.

"If you knew Chet was planning to kill me, why didn't you mention that little fact before we got here?"

This time, it was Barbara who chose to take the Fifth. He stared right through her for a long second, long enough to x-ray her soul with those penetrating blue eyes. Because she'd been afraid he'd back out, that he wouldn't help her. He knew without her saying it. The guilt that she refused to feel rose to bring a flush to her cheeks, but her fiercer maternal instincts gave a firm tip to her jaw. She wouldn't apologize. He sighed and shrugged it off.

"I guess it doesn't matter. I'm here now, and it's time Chet and I got things settled between us."

"He said we had thirteen days," she blurted out, as if that was reason enough to risk his life.

"And you believed him? After he killed Rob, you'd just take his word on that?" he asked matter-of-factly, without malice. Still, his question cut to the bone.

"I didn't have any choice."

"There are always choices, Barbara. It's the decisions that are up for grabs. You made yours. Just see that you can live up to it." He checked his watch. "We've got a bus to catch."

Ticktock.

An entertaining tour guide filled them in on all sorts of titillating bits of gossip as he deftly maneuvered the big bus down the confusing connection of streets. The seats were only half-filled by a group of high schoolers on an educational field trip, weary parents trying to direct bored youngsters, attentive older couples and several somber-faced veterans. Instead of taking the spot next to her in the plush touring coach, Tag opted for the other side of the aisle, several rows back. He'd forgone the dark glasses, replacing them with a ball cap tipped low enough to shield his features. A man who wasn't terribly interested in taking Chet Allen's word that an assassin's bullet wasn't in store for him. Barbara applauded his caution.

Their first stop was the World War II Iwo Jima Memorial. As their group circled it, Barbara realized she hadn't expected it to be so large…or to feel so moved by the heroic depiction. As their guide identified the soldiers involved in planting the flag, her attention slipped away, toward trying to identify another in their group who had cause to harm them. Then they were back on the bus and headed for the Jefferson Memorial.

She wandered there beneath the glorious dome, impressed by the gleaming, almost eerily glowing pillars that revealed peekaboo glimpses of the cherry-blossom-lined Potomac and a distant Monticello. While others drifted down to the air-conditioned gift shop, she remained on the pristine marble steps, anxious and obvious in her search of the surroundings.

"You won't see him unless he wants you to," came McGee's quiet comment. He stood on the opposite side of one of the pillars, just a tourist absorbed by the view. Or at least that's what any casual observer would think. "This is too wide-open for him to make a move. Relax."

As if that were possible.

Their next stop was the Mall and the Lincoln Memorial, where the rest of their group climbed the oddly spaced and well-worn steps to stand before Honest Abe where he sat overlooking the tall spire of his fellow president. She'd started up after them and then noticed that McGee had broken off, heading instead toward the sheltered trees where the Korean and Vietnam wars were remembered. After a second's hesitation, she hurried after him.

The Wall. She'd seen it in photos and on TV but was in no way prepared for the throat-tightening scope of it. Starting low, it escalated in size as the passing years brought more and more casualties to list in grimly precise rows. Rows that went on forever. These were the names of those who'd stood beside Robert, Chet and Tag, men who may have shared their rations, their stories, their fears. Gone, but not forgotten.

Her eyes began to fill at the sight of a wheelchair-bound man holding a flag in one hand while the other rested upon the cool stone. His head was bowed, his cheeks were damp. Families clustered together, dabbing at their eyes while taking tracings of their loved one's names eternally etched in history. Others stood before the text where they could look up their husbands, fathers, brothers and friends, to find their positions on the Wall. The mood was respectful and overwhelmingly quiet. She fought down the fullness in her throat as she saw Tag standing alone, scanning the roll call in heaven for the year 1972. He started to reach out, fingers unsteady, then drew back to fist them at his side. He felt rather than saw her behind him.

"So many good men," he stated softly, remorsefully. "So many good friends."

Barbara couldn't speak. She didn't know what to say, how to express her sorrow for what she hadn't experienced and couldn't begin to imagine. Robert never spoke of his tour, a tour he'd returned from with a wound that made him marketable for a political career. Coward that she was, she never asked him what he'd seen or done. Or what had happened to his friends. Now she wished she had. She wished she had some knowledge to guide her unfocused grief, so she could try to understand this isolated man with her and the one who stalked them in the shadows. But before she could make contact with her instinctively outstretched hand, McGee moved on, circling wordlessly and dry-eyed to the lesser known—but often cited as the most moving—memorial.

In the dimming light, they rose like the ghosts they were on a timeless march through enemy territory. The heroes of Korea. A chill traced along her arms at the stunning visual as she walked silently past their frozen unit to a wishing well and flanking wall. Upon that gleaming surface, faces instead of names were etched, representing those who'd served bravely, honorably and sometimes fatally. Up ahead, she could see the tension in Tag's stance. He was on full alert now in this more secluded spot. But still, Allen made no move.

The path led them by the statue immortalizing wartime nurses and Tag paused there for a moment to look up at their earnest faces, to smile, to nod his thanks. And then they were back on the crowded walkways where veterans' groups and souvenir hawkers elbowed for a prime spot to get noticed in booths, ranging from offerings of professional organizations to crates displaying shrapnel and enemy memorabilia.

"Excuse me, ma'am."

Weary, edgy and unwilling to be petitioned by another needy soul seeking a handout, Barbara began to walk faster as if she hadn't heard. Then, with a sigh, she stopped and turned toward the voice.

He was ragged and unkempt but his worn uniform was immaculate and proudly borne upon thin shoulders. His features were deeply etched with the signs of hard times and unfortunate choices. But his gaze was direct and held recognition, as if he had singled her out purposefully in the crowd.

"Yes?"

"Excuse me, ma'am, but a fellow asked if I would watch for you and give you this."

She looked down to see what he held in one almost skeletal hand. She tried to draw a breath, but suddenly there was no air to be had to fill her starving lungs. She tried to speak, but her vocal cords were unresponsive.

"Ma'am? Are you all right?"

She couldn't answer. She could only stare at what winked and glittered in his outstretched palm. It wasn't some medal or memento he meant to sell her. It was so surprisingly personal that she couldn't take it from him.

"Barbara?"

She tore her gaze from the offering to appeal to McGee with a tear-brightened look. His features closed down tight and grim as he snatched the bauble from his fellow veteran and demanded, "Where did you get this?"

Startled, the man stammered, "From a guy who gave me ten dollars to pass it to the lady."

"What did he look like?"

Rattled now, the vet shook his head. "Just a guy. I don't know. I didn't really get a look at him. Just at the cash. I'm sorry. I didn't know I was doing anything wrong."

Tag pressed his arm and then pressed an extra twenty dollars into the man's palm. "It's okay. Don't worry about it."

Then he turned to Barbara, who was as pale as the Korean soldiers.

"Barb, what is this?"

She glanced at the piece of jewelry, remembering the way it sparkled on the lapel of someone not accustomed to wearing precious stones. It had been a wedding gift, her peace offering to Tessa.

"It's my daughter's brooch. She was wearing it last time I saw her."

Chapter 4

"It doesn't mean anything," Tag told her for the dozenth time as they sat before relatively untouched meals at the hotel restaurant. "It doesn't mean he harmed her."

"Then how did he get this?" she demanded, her insistent gaze as glittery as the pin clutched in her hand.

"Bump and grab, most likely. She probably never missed it."

How could he sit there so unconcerned? Sobs quivered in her voice. "I want to call her. I have to know she's all right."

"If he's here, he can't be a threat to them there."

She knew what he said made sense, but she was thinking on an entirely different level. "Unless he's already done what he threatened to do."

"There's no percentage in that." Tag remained unblinking in the face of her distress. "Call her. But not from your cell. Use the public phone over there by the restrooms. Where I can see you."

She vaulted from her seat, pausing only when McGee gripped her wrist. His touch was warmer than his words.

"Be careful what you say. He may have someone else watching them."

She nodded. She hadn't thought of that. Calmer now, she crossed the crowded room and fished coins from her purse to plug into the slots. Taking a stabilizing breath, she punched in the numbers. The cell rang and then a crisply professional voice came on.

"You've reached Tessa Chaney. I'm unavailable to take your call. Please leave a message."

Barbara hung up. What kind of message could she leave? Forcing down the wildly frightening images her panic etched upon her mind, she made herself think slowly, clearly. And she dialed again.

"Personal Protection Professionals."

"Michael?" Calm. Calm. "It's Barbara. How are things going?"

"You interrupted a rerun of *Family Guy* to ask me that? Things are fine. Don't you trust me?"

The retired police detective would expect her to laugh, so she did before asking, "Have you heard from Tessa? I've only been able to get her voice mail."

"Yeah, she called today wondering the same about Jack. You guys need a social secretary. I know, that's why you have me."

She curbed her impatience to ask, "Is she coming

home tomorrow?" Please, please. Once she knew they were in the safety of Jack Chaney's fortress in the northern Michigan woods, she wouldn't have to worry so much.

"Change of plans, I guess. One of the other chaperones and some of the kids came down with some kind of stomach thing and are in the hospital. Nothing serious," he was quick to reassure her, "but they wanted to do some testing to make certain it wasn't contagious."

"But Tessa and Rose?"

"Are fine. They're treating the quarantine in their hotel room like playing hooky. And guess who that leaves on the hook? Yours truly. A day or two at most, was what the doc told them. They have to get the results from the CDC."

Centers for Disease Control? Her panic level surged to new heights.

"Just a precaution, Barb. There doesn't seem to be a health risk to the kids. The specialists just can't pinpoint the cause of the symptoms and until they figure it out, they're going to be under wraps. Just hospital protocol."

She wasn't reassured. Chet had gotten to them. She was sure of it, just not sure how. He wanted to keep them away from familiar surroundings where they could be more easily protected. So he could continue to use them for his intimidation.

"Where's Jack?" It was time to tell Jack. If anyone could keep his family safe, he could. He'd taken down Allen once before, breaking through the window of her husband's high-rise office to do so like the type of larger-than-life screen star hero he resembled with his swarthy good looks. He'd taken Allen down, but not out. He wouldn't make that mistake again. Jack Chaney was the kind of man who learned fast from his errors; if he didn't, he might not live to regret it. He understood Allen, the same way he'd understand Tag. She could trust Jack with her life and Tessa's.

Then came the bad news from Michael.

"He's still incommunicado."

"How about Russell?" Jack's urbane British friend was equally competent, equally lethal when the situation warranted it.

"He had another surgery on his hand this morning. I think the new missus is looking forward to chaining him up in the bedroom for a couple of days so he can recuperate. Or at least, that's what she was calling it." Then the elder Chaney's tone sobered. "Barb, is there something going on that I should know about? Something Stan and I can help you with? We can be handy for old crippled guys, you know."

"I know, and thanks," she said huskily. "It's nothing. Really. Just an unexpected reunion that has me a little emotional. You know how those things are."

"Booze and easy women?"

She laughed, easing the tension. "Jeez, I hope not."

"Do you want me to have Tess call you?"

Yes. Yes, please. She craved the sound of her daughter's voice the way she did her next breath. But, instead, she said, "No. I'll be out of reach for a while. Let her know I'll call as soon as I can. And Michael, thank you."

"That's why I get the big bucks, Barb."

She was so fortunate to have these wonderful, loyal friends that Jack Chaney had brought into her family.

A family she would keep together no matter what risks she had to take. No matter what challenges she had to face.

The biggest risk at that moment was seated at her table. In trusting him to stick by her. And the challenge was in the big bed in the room they shared. What were they going to do about that? She approached the table warily, too weary to master the whirring emotions threatening to blow the top off her control. Taggert McGee waiting for her. At one time, it would have been a dream come true. Now was not that time.

Meeting his penetrating gaze, Barb shook her head. A tremendous ache began to build there. The thought of confronting McGee and the untouched meal transformed her steady pulse into a dull, persistent throb.

"Do you mind if we just get out of here?"

Wordlessly, Tag tossed down a couple of bills to cover the check and rose to follow her to the door.

The press of his fingertips at the small of her back came as a surprise. As big a surprise as the sudden heat that radiated from that casual contact in seismic waves. So much warmth from such an innocent gesture.

What would it be like to sink into the curl of his embrace? Her system shivered at imagining it. If she turned to him and stepped in close, would he take her in his arms? Or would he stand there stiff and unyielding, denying her comfort the way he was denying her a sense of security? The risk of his rejection was just too great. And the chance of his acquiescence was more than a little scary to a woman who'd been so long out of the dating pool that the thought of dipping in a toe to test the water had her trembling with alarm.

Before she could consider the ramifications of that touch, it was gone. She found she missed the way the brief caress had scrambled her senses, making her feel all womanly and wanted for the first time in a long time.

How was she going to get over the hurdle of that big inviting bed when his slightest touch had her squirming?

She was grateful to leave the intimate dimness of the restaurant, where one could pretend to see what was not there. The stark lighting they stepped into left no such illusions. The lobby was filled with weekenders dragging their luggage behind them like reluctant pets on a short leash. It took them a moment to find a break to enter into the traffic flow. While they waited, Tag's ever-moving stare caught on the electronic bulletin boards announcing the events of the evening. Suddenly, he gripped her elbow with enough strength to make her gasp and propelled her forcefully into the path of a bevy of noisy New Jersey businesswomen who cursed him soundly for his rudeness. He didn't notice the language that made Barbara blush. Something had happened. Something she missed.

"What is it? McGee, what is it?"

But he wouldn't speak. His jaw gripped tight. His features were immobile granite, his eyes chips of blue ice. She had to trot to keep up with his purposeful strides.

Once inside their room, he released her. As she reflexively rubbed what could well develop into bruises, he hurried to turn on the television, flipping until he found the hotel channel. Cautiously, she moved to where she could view the screen. Meetings, registration times, group gatherings for the medical and realtor conventions at the hotel rolled by. Tag paid them no attention.

"There. There it is."

Reception for Phillip Frye, MD, in the ballroom at nine o'clock.

She glanced at Tag. "Doctor Frye. You know him?"

McGee's expression was all taut, haunted shadows. "He knows us, inside and out, you might say. He was the psychiatrist we saw when we came in from missions in the field. Our lieutenant insisted on it because of the jobs we were doing."

"As sharpshooters, you mean."

"As snipers," he clarified.

Barbara nodded. That was one of the few things she did know about what Robert had done in the jungles of Southeast Asia. He, Chet and Tag had parlayed their expertise with hunting rifles into the deadly role of government assassins. She could never picture Robert in that role that fit Chet so well and Tag more loosely. It was hard to imagine college-aged boys purposefully taking lives when months before they were lounging in dorm rooms grooving to Hendrix and Creedence Clearwater Revival. How much harder to do than to imagine?

"So what did the doctor do for you?"

"Just routine. We'd come in and talk to him and he'd see we had our heads on straight before we'd go out again."

"And were they?"

"Most of the time, yes." That's all he would offer. His gaze was decades and continents away. After a moment of silent contemplation, his focus began to slowly sharpen until he said, "He's the reason we're here."

"Frye?"

"I think so. According to the TV, he's supposed to receive some humanitarian award at the Kennedy Center tomorrow night."

"Why would Chet want us to talk to him?"

"I guess we won't know that until we have that chat. Let's see what you brought in that garment bag."

The suggestion was so out of left field that it took her a second to come up with it. "You want to look at my clothes?"

"Frye has as eye for the ladies. You shouldn't have any trouble getting him to take you up to his room."

Her jaw dropped. McGee didn't notice. He was busy unzipping her bag. One by one, he drew out the dresses she'd hastily picked for the trip. Dazzle and distract, Chet had told her, so she chose what she thought would fit the bill. Sparkly, glamorous tea- and full-length gowns in a rainbow of pastels. From that delicate bouquet, he selected the one dark bud.

"This one."

She hesitated. She hadn't wanted to bring the dress. She'd always felt uncomfortable in it, but it had been in the same dry cleaner bag as the others, so in it went.

"Hurry up. You don't have much time."

She balked. "Why don't you just go down and talk to him yourself?"

"Because it's better that I not be seen."

"Why?" When he wouldn't answer, she read between the softly drawled words. "You deserted?"

That got through his stoic facade. He winced in denial. "No. Of course not. I was formally discharged. But I was supposed to meet with Frye and some of my other superiors for a debriefing and I sort of didn't show up." There was a volume to be read there, but he was a closed book. She couldn't…wouldn't believe he was involved in the same illegal business that finally caught up with Allen. Not the conservative Tag McGee she knew. But then, what did she know about this man? Nothing at all. Except that he kept his secrets more stingily than his smiles.

What wasn't he telling her? And how did that relate to the danger they were in?

Her brows arched. "And they didn't come looking for you?"

"Oh, they looked."

Chet apparently wasn't the only one who wouldn't be found unless he wanted to be. Had Tag been in hiding for all those thirty years? Was that why he hadn't contacted her? Was that why Chet had to use her to lure him from his anonymity? Too many questions and far too few answers. He had to give her something.

"Why did you skip the debriefing?"

"I guess I was just tired of following the rules."

That didn't sound like Tag, who was always the soul of honor and dependability. He'd been above deception or deceit, with nothing to hide. Or at least she'd thought so until that bus pulled out. Getting information from him now required a crowbar.

"And Frye was one of them that made them?" she prompted.

"He was somewhere in that pecking order."

His careful evasion set off alarm bells in Barbara's brain. "McGee, why do they want you killed?"

"Let's ask Frye."

He paced the bedroom trying to stamp out the emotions skittering just beneath the surface, like tiny creepy crawlies under his skin. After so many years, he thought he'd be ready to face these men again. But he was wrong. As wrong as he was about being prepared to confront the devastatingly lovely woman who emerged from the bathroom in record time.

The dress was worthy of celebrity red-carpet notoriety. Black, fluid and sexy as hell, its halter top left her creamy back and shoulders bare. The two sides of the bodice met at the wide sparkly waistband instead of at the modest middle, leaving peekaboo glimpses of the perfect curve of Barbara's breasts. A long, thin silver chain trickled between them. Baby-fine blond hair was caught up on one side in a diamond-studded comb to expose the slender column of her throat and the narrow rope of silver and diamond chips that swung from one ear. The usual light touch she used to apply her makeup had taken a dramatic turn, accentuating lids and lips in dark, sultry hues that suggested a man might dream of a delightful end to the evening. A soft tease of perfume hinted of other sensory pleasures. And there was nothing Taggert McGee would have liked more than to take that hint and this woman on the spot to rekindle those long-held dreams once more. She made him ache just looking at her. How bad would it hurt, then, to touch her?

"So what does this Doctor Frye look like?" she asked, turning to the full-length mirror with a critical frown to adjust her hair and her neckline. "I'd hate to pick up the wrong man."

McGee's gut clenched at that. "He'll be the sloppy drunk, boasting loudly in the middle of a circle of eager sycophants."

Her rouged lips pursed. "Wonderful. And how do you know he'll take me up on my offer?"

His gaze swept the length of her, front and back in the mirror. The disbelieving snort that escaped from him was flattering in its crudity. "I won't dignify that with an answer. Suffice it to say, you'll have more trouble getting him as far as his room with his pants still on."

She made another face at her reflection. "Terrific."

Telling himself he wasn't sending her to the wolves, Tag made a show of checking his watch. "He should be in the thick of that booze and those stories by now."

Barbara stiffened. *Ticktock.* She got the idea. Still, he didn't have to look so eagerly indifferent about the thought of her hustling a stranger. She hadn't been that perky seventeen-year-old flirting with boys for longer than she cared to remember and feared her skills were rusty. But, she thought ruefully, what she'd forgotten would certainly be compensated for by the plunging neckline of her gown.

Terrific.

"This shouldn't take long. Hopefully."

As she started to the door, she was surprised by the sudden warm circling of his fingers about her upper arm. Just that brief touch made her go all hot and cold inside. Schooling her expression to betray nothing of the chaos ricocheting within the walls of her heart, she glanced over her shoulder. His chiseled features were solemn with a gratifying concern.

"Don't take any chances. And be careful."

His unexpected sentiment gave her the courage to be flippant. "Don't worry. I've handled my share of society inebriants."

His gaze shuttered. Of course, she had. And knowing that, it was easier to let her go.

The elevator was crowded with noisy partygoing conventioneers. She had to squirm to the back to make room for several others from her floor. Squashed into that haberdasher's mix of sequins and satins, she took a moment to get her game face on. Social mixers were her forte. Everyone said so, from her late husband to the society pages.

Only they didn't see the price she paid to maintain that perfect front. Her palms were damp, her stomach knotted. Her knees were locked to prevent weakening as she repeated her oft-chanted internal mantra. *Don't let me embarrass myself. Don't let me say anything foolish. Remember to smile and breathe and laugh, but not too loudly. A well-bred lady never laughs too loudly.*

She could hear her father's voice inside her head drumming those all important lessons into his awkward preteen, who even at twelve was expected not to sully the family's image. Vital lessons for the future wife of a political candidate. Necessary lessons for a woman embroiled in what was rapidly becoming a more complicated and dangerous intrigue.

"Nice dress."

It was too elbow-to-elbow for her to turn around to verify the identity of the man speaking quietly next to her ear. As if she needed to. The sound of his voice paralyzed all her major muscle groups.

"Don't look. Just listen," he continued with that same sinister softness.

She tried to silence the roar of blood pounding in her head by taking frantic gulps of breath.

"Remember, Babs, Frye is a professional liar. Don't pay attention to what he says, only to why he says it."

In spite of his instructions, she fought to revolve in the press of humanity, to confront him with her greatest fear.

"My daughter and granddaughter, are they all right?"

Just then, the doors opened and passengers spilled out, carrying her forward in the overwhelming flow. By the time she found her footing, the tide had swept past her. And with it, lost in that surge and swell, went Chet Allen.

He hadn't answered her.

The ballroom at the Wardman was indeed grand and opulent. Elaborate plasterwork, swirls of gilt and dripping crystals reflected endlessly in mirrored walls.

Barbara had no trouble locating Frye. Just as Tag predicted, the sobriety-challenged doctor held court circled by journalists and fawning admirers, enjoying his fifteen minutes of fame in high style. At week's end, he would be just another blip on the celebrity radar, hoping to hawk his memoirs to supplement his retirement. But for now he was sucking up the limelight with gusto. The same way he was slurping down the champagne.

Barbara drifted through the crowded room, nodding to those she passed as if they had reason to remember her. She lifted a flute from a passing tray to carry as a prop, knowing if she swallowed the contents she'd require more to bolster her unsteady nerves.

Then she latched on to the image of her daughter, Tessa, seated across from a killer, daring him to make a move. That was courage. This, this was necessity.

She knew when Frye's glazed stare touched on her. It felt like sweaty hands roving the length of her body in a clumsy, groping rush. She pretended not to notice as she paused just outside his surrounding wagons to look about with a bored air of impatience, as if she were waiting for someone and suspected she'd been stood up. Her dramatic sigh lifted her shoulders and did tempting things to her plunging décolletage to set the hook. As she started to move forward once more, she let the sway of her hips reel him in.

"What's a beautiful woman like yourself doing here alone?"

Fixing a smile upon her face that didn't display a hint of gloating, Barbara turned and feigned a delighted surprise.

"Doctor Frye. I didn't mean to take you from your audience."

"I always play better when the group is smaller, even intimate."

Her expression never wavered. "My name is Barbara D'Angelo. You knew my husband during the Vietnam era. He spoke very highly of the encouragement you gave him. In fact, he said you most likely saved his sanity and helped him continue in the rather unsavory work he did for our country at war."

Heavy white brows knit over a hawkish nose. She could visualize him mentally scanning his files. "Robert D'Angelo?"

"Yes. How flattering that you remembered. A man of your stature must have saved so many tormented souls over those awful years."

He drank in her flattery with the same appreciation he applied to the bubbly in his glass. "How is Robert?"

She let her gaze dip respectfully. "He's gone. Just six months ago."

He touched her arm in an outward show of sympathy. His fingertips grazed the back of it for an entirely different purpose. "I'm sorry for your loss."

She managed a heroic-sounding sigh. "That's why I was drawn to see you. After all, you and Robert had so much in common. Meeting you makes me feel close to him somehow."

With a casual flip of her hair, she landed him like a gasping trout, flopping at her feet.

Tag checked his watch. Forty-five minutes.

He paced the room, trying not to picture Barbara in that libido-busting dress revving up Frye's high-performance engine. Instead, he forced himself to consider why Chet would push him and the good doctor together for this carefully staged reunion. And that meant looking back, back over thirty years to a past as shadowy as the missions they conducted. To memories as shrouded with mystery as the assignments they completed. As vague as his recall of the sessions under Frye's care.

Why couldn't he remember? His entire tour was in vignettes. Bits and pieces that never connected into a satisfying story. Faces, places, all blurring by like a flip book, giving him glimpses but no substance. Something was very wrong about that. About him. Why couldn't he grasp one clear memory out of that cold, veiling fog enveloping his brain?

He'd gotten close. Sometimes in dreams, he could almost, almost reach behind that heavy curtain, but then he'd hear a familiar voice saying a nonsensical phrase, something seemingly innocuous yet with the power to plunge his thoughts into darkness. And he'd wake feeling sick to the soul with confusion. And afraid. Afraid of what that drape of forgetfulness concealed. Afraid it was madness. That's why he'd run away. That's why he'd made himself so hard to find.

Don't pay any attention to that man behind the curtain.

Who was there? Who was at the controls? Was it Frye? Or was it some part of himself that he didn't dare recognize?

What had he done? What had they made him do that was so awful that his own mind hid it from him?

He heard them in the hall and shifted instinctively

into stealth mode. Stepping back into the dressing
alcove, he waited for the door to open, for the giggling
Barbara to lead the doctor inside.

And then the sound of his voice, so smoothly comforting, like a tender brush of cool fingertips across a
fevered brow. Some mechanism in his mind reacted to
it without him knowing why. His stance relaxed, his
spirit calmed as if his tone was a narcotic balm to
Tag's system.

"You are a lovely and generous woman, Barbara.
Too much so to be alone at a time like this."

The crooning syllables lapped over the edges of his
consciousness, quieting his thoughts, slowing his
heartbeats. Mesmerizing, like a flute to cobra.

Then he heard Barbara's crisp reply. He blinked
awake from the daze he'd sunk into.

"I'm afraid I'm also deceptive and rather desperate.
And I'm not alone."

Chapter 5

Phillip Frye looked as if he'd seen a ghost. Finally, he was able to gather enough wits about him to murmur, "McGee, we've been looking everywhere for you."

"So I understand. What I don't know is why."

Frye backpedaled and sat heavily on the edge of the bed. His reason for coming up to the room was, apparently, forgotten as he stared at this unexpected specter from his past.

"Why? You know why. You and Allen were out on sensitive missions behind undefined lines for months. The next thing I know, you're stateside without bothering to check in or make a report. I don't know what strings you pulled, McGee, but you broke about every rule you can think of."

"Is that why you've been after me? To slap my wrist for breaking the rules? My time was up. I wanted to go home. I followed all the protocols I was required to and I left. I don't see the problem."

Barbara watched the interplay with interest. Tag was all cold control, while Frye's mind spun behind his placating expression. Something beyond the words they spoke was going on between the two men. What, she suspected, had everything to do with the difficulties they were in.

Frye smiled with a condescending kindness. "You know as well as I do that what you were involved in went beyond ordinary protocol. You and Allen, and for a time, D'Angelo, were vital to our operations over there. There were no rules governing what you did."

"You mean murder in the name of democracy?"

Frye flinched slightly. "You know that's not true. You did delicate and decisive work for our cause. That kind of task takes a toll on a man's psyche. We just wanted to make sure you were all right."

"Robert came back a hero and a statesman. Chet came home a psychotic. Did you want me to check in so you could see which way I was going to fall? Or were you afraid if I fell to pieces, your reputation would be tarnished? The way it would be if Chet was ever connected to your tender loving care? What are you afraid of, Doc? Of what I might do? Or what I might say?" Since he didn't look too concerned about either of those things, Tag took a chance.

"Or of what I might remember?"

Bingo.

An overly anxious Frye began to overcompensate with words. "You men witnessed and executed events that the average mind wasn't meant to hold and remain stable."

"We were doing our jobs," McGee stated carefully. "What exactly was your job, Doc? What did you do beyond slapping a mental bandage on before sending us back out into the thick of it?" He watched Frye's gaze go flat with fear and dread. And his own anxiety peaked as he whispered, "What did you do to us?"

Unexpectedly, the way they always seemed to come, one of those fragmented memories flashed in front of him. Stained canvas above, closing over him like the lid on a pressure cooker. The heavy smell of heat and rot and sweat. The uncomfortable tautness of a cot beneath him. Something dazzling before his eyes. So bright, he couldn't look away. A familiar cadence, not words, but rather a tone humming like a tuning fork through his head. Pulling at his eyelids. Weighting them like sandbags. Dragging them down. Then the blackness, so deep, so still, so empty, before an abrupt jerk back to the sight of that shadowed canvas. The cold, cloying fear that he'd missed something. Something more vital than just minutes.

What the hell had been done to him during those moments of disconnection?

"I helped you go back out there. I erased the horrors before they got too big to handle."

"Erased?" Barbara edged into the conversation. "How? With drugs?" She was thinking of what her husband had died to expose: a drug-trafficking ring that continued long after the troops had returned home.

"Nothing like that," Frye assured her. "Just mild antidepressants. For post-traumatic stress. I used a form of posthypnotic amnesia, mostly, to make events stored in long-term memory inaccessible. Light suggestions to tuck the brutality of your jobs back into the far recesses of your thoughts so you wouldn't have to deal with it every day. The men in your occupation suffered from reexperiencing phenomena. Nightmares, flashbacks, emotional detachment and sleep disorders that made it impossible for them to function normally."

"What was normal about what he did?"

"Nothing. And that's my point. I put false memories in place of what was causing so much anxiety."

"You were in our minds?" That was a horror greater than any they had sought to protect him from. "Who approved that? Who authorized you to tamper with our heads?"

"It was to help."

A terrible sickness twisted in his belly. Help? He thought of the night sweats and the clammy blanks of conscious thought. And the always-present feeling that a very, very bad something had just happened by his hand. Not knowing what it was. Not knowing who to ask. Or what to do about it. Followed by the cold, hard brilliance of Chet's grin.

Chalk up another one, Mac.

Madness. It had been madness. Chet embraced it zealously, like a new religion. How far over the line had they been convinced to go?

"I can see it really helped Chet Allen out."

At Barbara's harsh summation, Frye had the decency to squirm a bit. But not enough to imply true conscience. "Allen had issues of his own that I wasn't aware of at the time. If we'd known, we never would have used him."

"But when you found out, you didn't stop, did you?" McGee challenged. "Because he was too good at what he did. At what we did."

Barbara's attention shifted. "Is that why Robert never talked about what happened over there? I thought he just wanted to put it behind him. But you're saying he couldn't remember."

"Didn't want to, couldn't, those are very close sentiments," Frye explained. "So in Rob's case, it was easy for the suggestions to take root. He didn't want to be there doing what he was doing. He was focused on his life after Vietnam so it wasn't difficult for his mind to blank out his experiences and move on."

Barbara wasn't sure whether she should slap him or thank him. But Tag had no confusion there. He stepped up to get nose to nose with the doctor.

"What else did you do while you were in there? What other ideas did you plant?"

Frye put up his hands in blameless supplication, playing the beneficent humanitarian to the hilt. "I was just trying to help." Then the biggest cop-out of all. "I was just following orders."

"Whose orders?" McGee barked. "I want to know who gave the orders. Did they come from the Battalion HQ? From Sniper HQ in Dong Tam?

From some stateside bureaucrat playing with our lives like we were chess pieces?"

"I don't know. They came down through channels. I don't know where they originated. McGee, that was over thirty years ago. Why does it matter?"

"Someone thinks it does. The someone who wants Chet to kill me. What do you know about that, Doc?"

The man grew even paler. Perspiration trickled down to his starched collar. "I'm just here to accept an award and turn a book deal if I'm lucky."

"Then why did Chet want me to look you up?"

That notion brought a glaze of fear to his eyes. Rightfully so. "Allen's crazy. You know that as well as I do. Who knows what goes on in his mind?"

"You do, Doc. Or at least, you did. What did you put in there while you were poking around where you didn't belong? What did you do to push him over the edge? How did you just cut out that part of him that had a conscience? What did you do to make him into the kind of man who could put a bullet in his best friend without blinking an eye? You took away his soul. What do you think that kind of information would do to your prospective book deal? What kind of humanitarian makes it easier for a man to commit murder? I thought we went to war back in the forties to stop that sort of thing."

Frye's shoulders squared with indignation, righteous or not. "I did nothing wrong. I only tried to ease the mental suffering of men in combat. I'm not responsible for Chet Allen. Or for you. Now, I think I'd like the both of you to leave before I call hotel security."

He pushed himself up off the edge of his bed, but he was hardly an imposing figure when standing next to McGee, the fierce killing machine he'd helped create. His ego gave him the bravado needed to hold his ground. But it was McGee's choice to back down, to back away from this man who'd chopped a hole in his past and left him to wander through that void alone.

"We're not finished, Doc."

Frye suddenly shifted tactics. becoming all compassion and concern. "Come see me, McGee. Officially. I can help you. I can give you the same kind of peace of mind that D'Angelo found. I can make it so you can be…"

"What? Whole again? So I can forget what I did, who I was, and who was responsible? So I can let you off the hook? Help me what?"

"Put an end to the pain I see in your eyes."

Tag stepped back, momentarily taken off guard by that intuitive statement.

"We have unfinished business," Frye continued, his tone silken and convincing. "That's why I needed to see you one last time before you went stateside. That's why you're so confused now."

"I'm fine," Tag hissed through gritted teeth. "I don't need any more of your help. But I will find out the truth."

With that dire vow, he stalked from the room. As Barbara started to follow, Frye caught her arm. His voice was low with urgency.

"Make sure he comes to see me. He needs someone to put the pieces back together for him. All he has are fragments now. The post-traumatic stress disorder is causing high anxiety levels. It's that hyperarousal and avoidance behavior that makes this idea of a conspiracy believable. If someone else is responsible, he can remain in that numb state indefinitely. He needs help, whether he'll admit it or not. Until he gets it, he's in a fight or flight mode. And he could be…dangerous. Dangerous to himself and those around him."

Barbara's disbelief was plain. "Tag McGee would never harm anyone."

"Maybe not the man you knew. He's not that man anymore, Mrs. D'Angelo. He's what we made him. Him and Allen both." He pressed his card into her hand. "Call me. Set up an appointment. My office staff will be expecting you and will give you priority. Just please, do it soon. Please take me seriously."

She remembered looking into Chet Allen's emotionless eyes while he smiled at the thought of her death.

Oh, she took it seriously, all right.

And she nodded, pocketing the card.

She expected him to be waiting for her outside Frye's room, but he wasn't. Nor had Tag returned to her suite. The corners were quiet, the shadows deep. She undressed quickly without the lights and then barricaded herself in the bathroom with her chaotic thoughts.

The stinging heat of the shower couldn't warm her.

He's what we made him. Him and Allen both.

What did that mean? What the *hell* did that mean? That she was in the middle of a tug-of-war between two deadly madmen? Two men so mentally damaged and out of control that their own government handlers would seek to destroy them? Or was it the knowledge they carried that made them so dangerous? How much of the perceived threat was real and how much imagined?

She turned off the spray and stood shivering in the heavy mist of steam that clouded the bathroom the way this whole situation shrouded her emotions.

How was she going to get her family out of this quagmire alive?

Struggling to rein in the hysteria that raced beneath the surface of her hard-won calm, she towel dried her hair with shaking hands and avoided her reflection in the all-seeing mirror where she was just a vague shape without substance. Like Taggert McGee.

What did she really know about the man he'd become? More than thirty years had passed. Thirty years. During that time, Robert had built himself a prestigious career in the law just as Chet had established a reputation by circumventing it. What had Tag been doing? What deadly game drew them here, these two skilled assassins and the memory of her husband, making her and her loved ones disposable pawns? How could someone as ill-equipped as society arm candy hold her own, let alone prevail? Yet she would have to if she wanted back that new life she'd just begun to enjoy.

Belting her robe about her waist, she stepped out into the dark bedroom, pulling up short with the brightness from the bathroom spotlighting her. A deer in headlights. For a moment, she stood frozen, her heart hammering within her chest until she realized that the figure standing just out of the reach of the light was not Chet Allen. But in that fleeting instance of doubt, all her fears, all her inner terrors must have been displayed upon her face because Tag McGee spoke to her quietly, with an undertow of melancholy pulling on every word.

"You know I would never hurt you, Barbara."

The pain of his long-ago abandonment lanced through her with an unexpected savagery. She couldn't respond.

"I'm not like Chet," he continued with a determined forcefulness, as if his one mission in life was to make her believe that. "You know I never could be. You know me better than anyone else. You remember who I was, what was important to me."

She heard herself reply in a leaden voice, "That was a long time ago."

"But you still remember, don't you?" He sounded almost desperate for that assurance and suddenly she wished she could see his expression, to read what was in his eyes. "You remember who I was and what we were to each other."

"Yes." Barely a whisper. How could she forget? The anguish of those emotions was as fresh as yesterday.

"I need you to tell me," was his startling request. "Because I don't remember." He ran an unsteady hand through thinning hair. "I mean I do, but it's like a dream, like it might not really have happened, or that it happened to someone else and I was just watching."

She was too stunned to react. At her hesitation, he

came forward, into the cool gleam of the fluorescents. The angles of his face were all dramatic highs and lows, his pale eyes fired with a haunted intensity. She was mesmerized by him, the same way a silly young girl had been.

"The last clear memory I have is of you."

Still, she didn't know what to say, so he continued in that low, tortured tone.

"I have thirty years of shadows in my mind. The image of you at that bus station is the last thing that stands out as real. The rest is like a fog I've been wandering through, not really knowing where I've been or what I've been doing. Sometimes, I'm not sure…"

She took an involuntary step back. That defensive response woke him from his pensive speech. He laughed, a soft, slightly embarrassed apology.

"I'm sorry to sound so *Twilight Zone.* I'm scaring you." His voice lowered and he glanced briefly away. "I'm scaring myself. It's just that I didn't realize how strange things have been until just now. It feels like I've been sleepwalking through the years without even knowing it. Now I'm awake and wondering where I've been."

"Where have you been?" Her request was hesitant enough to make him shake his head and smile.

"I know where I've been. I don't want you to get the wrong impression here. I'm not Looney Tunes or anything like that." But his voice faded out for a moment, as if he were questioning the validity of that claim.

"Where have you been?" she asked again, more

assertively because suddenly, it was very important
that she know. She wanted that answer, not just
because of this situation but because she needed to
know how he'd filled those years she'd hoped to share
with him. To know that what had been more important to him than her and the child he'd never acknowledged. That need to know wedged up into her throat
on razor-sharp points, refusing to go up or down. He
owed her that much honesty.

"When I left the service, I just wanted to get away.
from everything and everybody. To someplace quiet,
someplace…"

Safe. Safe was what he meant to say but didn't
because he wasn't sure why that word had come to
mind. And because Barbara was already looking at
him as if he were some kind of wacko who'd just
slipped the buckles of his restraints. He didn't want to
give her any further reason for alarm. He needed her
to believe in him just now. That wouldn't happen if he
unburdened all his ghosts upon her. How could a
delicate, sheltered woman like Barbara Calvin
D'Angelo understand, let alone cope with, the horrors
that crept through his past in nightmares that woke him
on the edge of a scream with disturbing frequency?
How could he explain what he'd experienced, the
numb sort of limbo he'd drifted through, without rightfully losing her trust? How could he get her to believe
it wasn't PTSD, the way Frye insinuated? It was something else. Something worse. He took a stabilizing
breath and tried again.

"I needed peace, Barbara. I needed a place where

I didn't have to think or feel or remember." But that was the funny thing. He couldn't remember. He couldn't remember any of those years he'd escaped, not with any certainty. Then the greater truth. "I needed a place to heal."

And he'd needed a place to hide. From the confusing unknowns that stalked the perimeters of his mind like silent sentinels. From the fear that he hadn't come back as the decorated hero everyone thought him to be, but as something else altogether.

"And you couldn't come to your friends to help you with that?"

Hurt vibrated through her quiet accusation.

"No."

There was no kind way to put it. And there was no way to tell her the truth. That he couldn't stand the thought, let alone the sight, of her and his best friend living out the dreams he'd held of their future.

"So where did you go?"

Grateful to escape her previous question unscathed, he told her, "Odd jobs. Traveling around." Hard to get a lock on. "Eventually, I took a job as a forest ranger on Isle Royale up in Lake Superior. I've been there these past seven years."

And in the wilds on that nearly deserted island, afloat on cold, unforgiving waters, living alone, without pressures, without demands, he'd existed simply, day to day. He didn't have to face reminders of the ugliness of a war that had left untold and unimagined scars on his two best friends, one lost to inner demons unleashed within the jungles and the other to the woman he'd loved but apparently wasn't good enough to keep. At least, until he slept at night.

Barbara frowned, her quick mind picking up on a flaw in his reasoning. "How could they not find you if you were living in a national park? Wouldn't the government have records of you being an employee?"

"If that was the name I'd given them, yes."

"You're living under an assumed identity?" Suspicion and a hint of fear colored that question.

"After the official conflict was over, I was still there, working for the government, Barbara. You get to know people. You get to call in favors. I called in a big one. Once I got discharged, I told a buddy of mine that I wanted to disappear and he made it happen."

I know a guy who knows a guy. She could hear Jack Chaney casually explaining away his web of deadly contacts spun between the cracks of military intrigue.

"So how did Chet find you?"

"I gave him an emergency number, a way to contact me indirectly in case he needed me."

That sentiment burned within her breast. In case Chet needed him. But no such consideration for her or their child. If Robert knew his whereabouts, he'd never told her. Taggert McGee had been an off-limits subject between them. Just the way she and Tessa must have been an out-of-mind, out-of-heart sort of thing for Tag. The irony of Chet forcing this awkward reunion returned with renewed bitterness.

"Why now? Why wait all these years to reach out and touch you?" She spoke with a flat, almost disinterested tone that had McGee's brows furrowing slightly.

"Why are you suddenly such a danger that someone would threaten my family just so he could take you out?" She realized that sounded as if she was irritated at being drawn into this scheme for his demise, but she preferred that to his knowing how deeply his disregard wounded her.

He didn't miss the nuances in that question. His features tightened. His voice chilled. "I regret that. I really do. I would never have involved you or Rob's daughter. And I promise, I'll let no harm come to either of you. I owe that to Rob."

To Robert? What about what he owed to her? For all the pain of broken promises, all the anguished nights alone, all the fruitless trips to the P.O. box hoping for letters that never came. For leaving her when she'd been desperate and afraid and needed him most, forcing her to make the only choice available to protect her family and her unborn child?

Then a single unexpected fact threaded through the fabric of her indignant pain.

He'd said Robert's daughter. As if he didn't know Tessa was his child.

As if he didn't recognize that a huge wave of uncertainty and disbelief had just swept her legs out from under her, Tag continued, "Something's going on, right here, right now. And there's a reason Chet doesn't want me to miss out on it. If he'd wanted me dead, he'd have taken me out the second I stepped off that plane. No. There's more. Something I'm not getting. Something to do with Frye and why or what I can't remember."

"Why don't you take the doctor up on his offer? Maybe he can unlock your memories."

He waved off her faintly offered suggestion. "I don't think Frye wants to unlock anything. I think he'd prefer to have whatever's in here," he tapped his temple, "remain there. What's he so afraid of? That I'll ruin a book deal? If anything, that kind of controversy would make him a talk-show must-have. There's more at stake. Something they'd kill to protect."

"Who?"

"Them that makes the rules," he quoted grimly.

"Who made the rules, Tag? Chet said you'd know."

He shook his head. "I don't know. That's the problem. Either I never knew or Frye made sure I wouldn't remember." He paused, noticing the weary way Barbara was rubbing her eyes. "It's late and you're tired." She started to protest but he wouldn't hear of it. He was too chewed up inside to go much further himself. And he was on the verge of letting her see just how slender the thread of his control was.

"It's been a long day," he said at last, "and we're not going to solve this thing tonight. I've got a few ideas to follow up on tomorrow, so we might as well get some sleep before Chet deals us another card. Probably another joker." She didn't laugh. Come to think of it, he didn't think it was particularly funny, either.

As her glance darted toward the smooth surface of the king-size bed, he solved that dilemma with a firm, "I'll take the chair."

As McGee rechecked the locks on the door, Barbara

went to toss the damp towel in the bathroom and quickly, as nervous as a newlywed, donned the simple silk gown she'd brought to sleep in. Only at the time, she hadn't imagined she'd be sleeping with Taggert McGee. Well, not exactly with him... Her fingers trembled as she brushed out her hair. A fluster of emotions shook through her insides.

Sleeping with Tag McGee. Oh, how she remembered what he must have found all too easy to forget. How good, how right, they'd been together.

He'd levered out of his boots and dragged the coverlet off the bed before dropping into the armchair near the window. Without a word to her, he cocooned himself in the quilted folds of the bedspread the way he'd once nestled into her embrace and was asleep in the span of a heartbeat.

Leaving her standing there garbed in sexy pink silk and equally slippery doubts.

Finally, she moved to the big bed and slid beneath the sheets. She lay on her back for long, torturous minutes, her head and heart filled with the hush of Tag's even breaths. So long ago, a young girl had been mesmerized by those same sonorous sounds and by the man who uttered them.

How wildly, willfully she had loved him.

And then that single, shocking notion returned.

How could it be possible?

How could he not know that Tessa was his child?

Chapter 6

How could he not know?

Barbara lay in the darkness while that single question battered at her soul.

She'd discovered the unplanned pregnancy a month after the three of them left for boot camp. Maybe she'd suspected before, but she kept telling herself that it was just her upset over seeing them leave—seeing *him* leave—that had her system all out of whack. When a clinic test in another suburb confirmed it, she was shocked, afraid, but not truly devastated. How could she reject this piece of Taggert McGee that she carried within her body's embrace? They loved one another. She had no doubt that he would do the right thing without regret. They'd just be starting their family a bit sooner than planned.

It would be difficult. She wasn't sure she could count upon her parents' support. Her father was a respected circuit court judge and he'd seen far too many of Tag's relatives before his bench to think the youngest son would ever amount to anything. It didn't matter what she said or what Tag did to prove otherwise. Her mother, a child psychologist, should have taken Tag's side, having seen the investigative reports of abuse and neglect that always ended with the children placed back in the unstable McGee home. An unbonded child never learns how to return love, Claudia Calvin predicted and wrote him off as a bad risk.

But Tag knew about love and how to share it. He'd learned during the summers he'd spent as a child, when he'd escape the boiling pot of anger and alcoholism in his home to absorb the quiet balm of his grandfather's farm in rural southwestern Michigan. It was there he'd learned respect, devotion, pride and, most importantly, love. It had been his one haven until the old man passed away when Tag was thirteen. Then he found refuge in books. And finally with Barbara Calvin.

Barbara had had no doubts where Tag McGee was concerned. Not a single one. It would be rough, but they would make it. She wrote to tell him about her situation and then waited for a call, a letter, a card, planning to wed him when he came home on leave that Christmas before the baby began to show in her senior year at high school.

Nothing.

No response whatsoever.

Panic began to claw at her heart. Fear laced through her thoughts as the silence continued.

And then it was Robert D'Angelo who came home that Christmas, not Tag McGee. He was the one who heard her desperate plight and offered a solution.

She never heard from Tag. Never saw him again. Not since he'd stepped on that bus and out of her life. Away from his obligations. And her heart and faith had been broken.

How could he not know? Some mistake? Some miscommunication that unfairly pulled their lives in two different directions, leaving them both isolated and alone, him in the wilds of northern Michigan, her in the confines of an empty marriage? The magnitude of those thoughts played about in her mind like the mocking irony of some Shakespearian romantic tragedy.

Because her heart could no longer hold the possibility that circumstance, not intention, had kept them apart, when the first pinks of daylight colored the room she rolled toward the window to ask the questions that had tortured her for thirty years.

Why?

Why didn't you answer? Why didn't you come home?

How could you not know?

But he was gone.

The chair was empty of even his body's impression, as if he'd never been there at all. The coverlet was folded at the foot of the bed. She'd never heard him get up, let alone leave without a word.

And now she would have to wait, holding those questions close to a newly hopeful heart. Hoping for what, she didn't know. A new start? A second chance? Or just the opportunity to forgive and go on.

That would depend upon McGee's reaction to learning that Robert had fathered only their two sons. Tag was responsible for her eldest child, the daughter made between them, Tessa.

In the early morning hour, the Mall was without the throngs of tourists. Frisbee tossers and picnicking families would arrive later. Vendors had yet to set up their wares. It was still some sixty minutes before the first of many commuters would burst from the subway exits like a swarm of anxious ants from a disturbed hole.

It was there, next to one of those stations, that he hid in plain sight. He used the openness to his advantage so he had an unrestricted view while secreted in cloaking shadow. Then, right on time, a single figure emerged from the tunnel.

"Colonel Kelly?"

He was older, with gray muting the once fiery red of his hair, hair he still wore military short even though the combat drabs had long since been replaced by tailored suits. But the businessman attire couldn't distract from the immediately alert pose that came from a man who'd once lived with danger.

Tag's former CO regarded him with an instant welcoming smile.

"McGee, damned good to see you, son. Your call came as quite a pleasant surprise. I don't get the chance to see many from our old unit any more."

"Yes, sir. Good to see you, too, sir."

"It's not sir anymore. Just plain Mister." He patted his middle. "That comes with retirement, twenty extra pounds and three kids. Did you know I married Su Lee Quan? I run the States' side of her family's import-export business now."

"I hadn't heard that. Congratulations, sir."

Kelly sighed at the continued use of military respect but chose to ignore it. Ingrained habits died hard. He gave McGee a once-over, seeing little change from the toughly fit and mostly silent kid who'd been assigned to cover his rifle platoon. A few more pounds, a few more lines but the same unsmiling, get-right-to-business attitude. He and Allen were the sniper team, a shooter and a spotter, attached to his company as they went out on night operations, shadowing their patrols with their XM-21s, 3X9 Redfields and six-pound Starlight night scopes. They were called the unit's thirteen-cent killers because their rifle cartridges cost Uncle Sam thirteen cents each. At first the men steered clear of them because what they did sometimes came uncomfortably close to murder, but to a man, they always breathed easier knowing the two of them were in position on some distant ridge watching their backs.

"Are you here for Frye's big night, too?"

McGee hesitated.

Could he trust this man with his doubts, his concerns? It had been thirty years. But in looking at him, all that time melted away to one indelibly imprinted image. That of then Lieutenant Patrick Kelly in jungle fatigues waving them to follow. And they had. There wasn't one of them in his command who wouldn't have followed him into hell. And they had, hadn't they? He'd been a fair and competent leader who'd become a compassionate, caring friend. And he'd brought almost all of them home alive. Those he'd had to leave behind, he'd cried over without shame.

Still, McGee was cautious.

"You might say that, sir."

Kelly's gaze narrowed. He was familiar with McGee's conservative choice of words and was instantly suspicious. "But you didn't say that. What's on your mind, McGee? What brings you from wherever you've been holed up to call me away from my financial section this early in the morning?"

"Chet Allen."

All traces of relaxed retirement fell from Kelly's frame. He became flint and steel.

Kelly had been a mother hen to his men without exception, promising to watch out for them as long as they stood by him when it counted. Allen shied away from that companionable attention, preferring the company of his two buddies from home and his own tightly held counsel. Like McGee, he'd been on the receiving end of one too many harsh and scarring parental disciplines.

But where Tag appreciated a good man who deserved his allegiance, Chet distrusted all authority. He wasn't a follower and he didn't like rules. That put him and his CO on opposite ends more than once. But whatever differences they might have, they had stayed in the unit. No reports of misconduct ever made their way beyond those boundaries. Kelly took care of his own. And to a man, including a reluctant Allen, they respected him for it.

But once Allen left his command, scary things had trickled back the way scary things tended to. Rumors he hated to hear but couldn't dismiss.

"I thought he was on his way to prison." There was such regret and frustration in that brief statement. Such a waste, was what he didn't say. "What's he up to now? No good, I assume."

"He's here in D.C. It has something to do with Frye, but I'm not sure which side the good doctor is on."

"Neither am I. And that's one of the reasons I'm here."

"Sir?"

"What do you remember about Tam Quan, my wife's first husband?"

A sudden low hum started inside Tag's head. He blinked hard trying to discourage it. "He was your South Vietnamese counterpart."

"And he was assassinated along with his two young children while my wife watched. She recognized the man who killed them from a clip on the news a month or so ago, and she demanded justice for their unauthorized murders."

The buzz in his head rose to a roar. "Killed by whom?"

"Allen. I'm part of an investigation to link that killing to Frye. Apparently Frye was indulging in a little black market child slavery and Tam found out about it. Frye sent Allen to silence him and his family. Fortunately, Su escaped and is now more than willing to testify."

The sound had grown to the cacophony of hot summer cicadas, shrieking maddeningly between his ears. It was a struggle to maintain a straight face, pretending nothing was wrong. But something was. Something was very wrong. So he asked, "Why pull me into this?"

"Perhaps Frye thinks you know more than you're saying about his profit-making tour in 'Nam. Do you, son?"

It grew hard to breathe. Tension knotted in his belly until the need to retch was almost overpowering. Sweat, cold and slick, built on his brow. What did he know?

"McGee?"

Because he couldn't find an answer to what was asked, he found another question. "Who gave Frye the order to use hypnotism to mess with our minds? We sure as hell didn't agree to it."

The truth was worse than McGee expected.

"He was using hypnotic suggestion to send our men after nonmilitary targets, then erasing their memory of what they'd done to cover his own agenda."

"He was using Chet. And me." Icy cramps of nausea threatened to buckle his knees but he held firm against them. Was this Frye's handiwork, as well, this sudden physical distress? His means of getting Tag to back away from anything that might lead him in the right direction? He breathed hard into it, refusing to succumb.

"Not exclusively, but primarily. I'm sorry, son. I didn't find out about it until you'd already gone home. That's why I was trying so hard to find you. To make sure no permanent damage had been done."

McGee swallowed down the harsh laugh that would have sounded, well, crazy. Damage. His brain had been scrambled like a breakfast omelet. Kelly placed a bracing hand upon his shoulder, squeezing just firmly enough to snap him out of a nonproductive tailspin.

"I tried to take care of you," Kelly concluded.

Uncomfortable with talk about his own weakness, McGee took another path, one that held few pitfalls.

"Why does Frye want me dead? Rumor has it that Chet has a contract on me. Why? I don't remember anything."

"Are you sure? Are you sure there's no residual recall? Frye never got the chance to do that final memory wipe on you the way he did D'Angelo and others. Maybe that's why you're such a threat. He's afraid bits and pieces will come back to you. Maybe jumbled memories. Maybe in dreams. Things that might not make any sense to you. Anything like that, McGee?"

Tag stared him straight in the eye and shook his head. "No, sir. Everything is squared away up here." He tapped his temple and watched his CO give a sigh of frustration. Or relief.

"There is one thing, son," Kelly said carefully. "And I want you to think about this. Is there anything Allen might have said, anything you might have seen but just didn't connect? Anything strange or out of line?"

"About what, sir?"

"The children. Su's children. Their bodies were never found."

It was just a flash, a sliver of a second, like an image caught as channels were being changed. Two young faces, twisted in terror and wet with tears. The picture stabbed through his brain, a hot knife of pain and surprise. His rigidly schooled features betrayed neither. His tone was flat and neutral.

"I'm sorry, sir. I don't know anything about any children. The only targets I remember were military. Are you sure it was Allen?"

There was a soft puff of sound. Wood on the frame of the subway tunnel splintered in the space between them. A bullet.

Tag's gaze swept the perimeter. He put the shooter at eight hundred to a thousand yards out. Only one other man besides himself could have made such a shot. Chet Allen.

Patrick Kelly was gone, taking refuge back in the tunnel where no sniper shot could catch him. Instinctively, Tag faded back, as well, until his form was indistinguishable in the shadows. His mind was clear, the torturous pains gone.

Frye. Frye had sent them out to kill civilians. The anguish lancing through him wasn't falsely induced. Children. He tried to recapture their frightened faces but the image was gone, as if it had never existed either in dream or reality.

Which was it? The answer was just out of reach, playing hide-and-seek in the fog-draped recesses of his mind. A mind warped by Frye's direction.

If Chet had murdered children, had he been sent out to do the same level of evil without conscious knowledge of it? If he was seeing their fear-stricken faces, had he been a witness to that ghastly crime? Was that why Frye wanted him dead? Or had he become a rogue soldier, a mercenary like Allen, with Frye just trying to heal the tears in his psyche?

A dull throb began at the base of his skull.

How could he return to Barbara with these questions unanswered? How could he spend another night listening to the soft lure of her breathing without wanting to excite it to a quickened pace beneath him? How could he hear the shift and twisting of her body without rekindling the feel of those silken swells and tempting hollows moving against him, with him? The look in her eyes said she saw him as some sort savior, some hero come to rescue her from her fears.

What if he were as big a nightmare as Allen?

He turned from that train of thought. What he did or didn't feel or fear for Barbara wasn't what he needed to focus on. Not until the riddle Chet drew him into was solved.

Why didn't Chet want him talking to Kelly? He was no fool. If his friend had wanted either of them dead, they would be.

So, if Patrick Kelly was a wrong turn on the path Allen was coaching them down, which way was he supposed to go next?

And then he heard a whispered step behind him. Wondering how someone had managed to get the drop on him without him knowing it, McGee started to turn, his hand going for the pistol he wasn't supposed to be carrying. Then, words he could never remember afterwards whispered to him, coaxing him to drop his guard.

Kingdom come.

And everything went black.

* * *

"How are you enjoying D.C. so far, Babs?"

She'd pounced on the ringing phone, thinking it must be the inexplicably absent McGee. Hearing Allen's voice turned that expectation to alarm.

"Why are we here, Chet? I'm tired of this game. I want to go home to my family."

"Oh, but Barbie, we haven't even begun to play yet. What did you think of Frye? Did you believe him? What kind of reward do you think he really deserves tonight?"

"What did he do to you, Chet? To you and Rob and Tag?"

"He made us do unimaginable things," was Allen's soft, chilling response. "Things that would haunt my conscience, if he'd left me one."

"Is that why we're here? So you can clear your conscience?"

A pause, then Allen's easy laugh. "I sleep just fine at night. How about Mac? How's he sleeping these days?"

"How do you think, with your threats breathing down our necks?"

"Not very conducive to romance. Sorry about that, Babs. Not exactly the reunion you expected."

Her forceful expletive must have shocked him for there was a long silence before his sudden, silky confession.

"There was a time when that suggestion would have truly appealed to me. You had everything, Barbie doll. You had Robby and Mac and me wrapped around your fingers, so don't tell me you don't like to play games. Not when you're a master at it. You always did look down that pretty nose at me, the same way Robby did when it came right down to it. Both of you, the perfect spotless society pair. But we know better, don't we, Babs? You know all about secrets, how to keep them, how to use them to your best advantage. You know how to protect your own. That's why it's so much fun to have you in the game. You know what's at stake and you'll do anything to win."

"Who hired you to kill Tag? Does this have anything to do with Robert?" She was reaching, grasping for anything. Anything that would turn his taunting conversation away from the all-too-personal.

"Robby was business and pleasure. You see, he only pretended to be my friend. The minute my image got a little too discolored for his future plans, he turned on me, Barbara. The same way he turned on Mac to get what he wanted where you were concerned."

"What do you mean by that?"

Allen only laughed. "Ticktock, Barbie. There's a ticket at the front desk for you. It's to the good doctor's award ceremony tonight. Enjoy the show."

"Is Frye the one you're after? Or is he the one calling the shots?"

"Frye's a vain fool. But he's not an innocent one. Remember, not everything's business."

The line went dead.

Ticktock.

Chapter 7

Where was McGee?

In her shimmery copper-colored gown, Barbara fit right in with the glitzy crowd waiting outside the Kennedy Center in the sluggish pool of limos and tour buses. But her anxiety set her apart from the other gala-goers. She wasn't there to be entertained. She was there to be enlightened.

No word from Tag. She'd left a note in the room and could only hope he'd stop in long enough to read it. *Enjoy the show.* Was there something here to see beyond the production readying inside? Her head ached trying to figure out the twists and turns of Allen's merry chase. Was this just a way to get McGee in his sniper sites?

No word on Tessa. She'd left a message with Michael to have her daughter call her cell, but so far no contact. And Jack hadn't checked in with the office yet, either. Silence all around, leaving her stranded to pick her way through the sticky web of intrigue Chet was luring her into by herself. To what purpose?

She moved down the sidewalk with the flow of invitees, pulled past the giggling group of young people examining the frieze with its rather graphic homoerotic poses and across the vehicle-plugged street. Then she heard an odd sound above the traffic and chatter. As a child of the sixties, she knew it immediately. The sound of voices chanting in protest.

It wasn't a loud or unruly group, but the cluster of Vietnamese moved down the sidewalk in a forceful wave. Their banners and signs were mostly in the characters of their own language but some declared their cause with screaming intensity.

Dr. Mengele deserves no honor.

Horror not humanitarian.

Where are our children?

As news crews greedily turned their cameras toward the controversy, Barbara caught sight of a face in the crowd. Her breath seized up.

In his neatly pressed suit, with his bland smile, Chet Allen didn't stand out as a psychopathic killer.

He was only visible for an instant, only long enough to make certain she saw him, before blending back anonymously into the push of ticket wielders.

The anxiousness already dampening her hands became a cold, icy glove of fear.

The curtain was about to go up on Allen's private play.

She sat through the evening of long-winded and often teary testimonials, capped by the presentation of Frye's humanitarian award. The doctor was suitably gracious and overwhelmed, but still managed to take advantage of every photo op. In the crowded main hall where attendees poured from the auditorium, he set up court to laugh and pose; as he did, the showman surpassed the humble philanthropist.

Then Frye's gaze lifted and the joke he was telling faded upon his lips as he saw Barbara in the hall. His attention darted about, scanning the balconies above. Looking for Chet or Tag, she was sure. Finding neither didn't reassure him for he nodded his thanks to the eager hangers-on and began to move toward the exit and the liquor- and babe-laced reception to follow.

What was he so afraid of? The souring of a book deal or something far greater?

She trailed after Frye's entourage as they left the building, pausing as he stopped outside for more pictures. As the doors opened, she could hear the protesters. Frye's effusive smile tightened ever so slightly but he never dignified their cause with a glance in their direction.

And then it was too late for him to recognize any cause, even his own, as he fell, killed by a single shot from above.

The sound, how could he ever forget it? The singsong cadence of voices from another world, another time.

As their number surrounded and swept by him, McGee's senses swirled. He breathed in the scent of jungle rot, sooty cooking fires and spicy stew, could hear the wail of babies and children crying, the barking of camp dogs. And over it all, the whooping of evac copter blades. A staccato of rifle fire, punctuated by screams of pain and fear, echoed through his head. He wanted to clap his hands over his ears, but he couldn't raise them from his side. He was helpless to react, to respond to the stampede of desperate chaos, followed by deathly silence. By death. He was sinking into it like quicksand. The harder he fought, the faster he was pulled under.

Someone bumped him, making him reach out to grab for purchase and sidestep to keep his footing. The blare of a horn brought his eyes snapping open. He was balanced on a curb about to step into traffic.

Where the hell was he?

He'd been at the Mall where the grass still glistened with morning dew. Chet had taken a shot at them, not to kill but to startle. He'd gone on instant alert until something snatched the moment away. A phrase spoken from behind him. What was it? What were the words that blew out his conscious thoughts like a match, leaving him in darkness?

It was dark now, a darkness filled with remembered feelings, those of panic, noise, flight. Something had happened behind him, something to incite that terror to escape in those who swarmed from the scene, pushing past him to get away from an unseen danger. It wasn't a memory. It was happening now.

He turned slowly. The sense of being in a dream state weighted his reaction time, the movement gradual to the point of lethargic. In comparison, every-thing around him was moving at double time. Finally, his focus fell upon a group gathered near the main exit...of the Kennedy Center? A figure was on the ground. Men with handguns were crouched low, scanning the area with hard professional eyes. The walk was stained a bright spreading crimson. Someone had been shot.

And he was standing less than one hundred yards away with a rifle in his hand.

He stared at it, the XM-21 with silencer, as sur-prised as if he'd grown a second hand. It was heavy as hell and good only up to about 300 yards. But it made no noise. It wasn't his. He hadn't held one in his hands since he'd left 'Nam. He didn't know where it had come from or how it had gotten into his grip.

Then it all clicked together like the clink-clank of an ejected cartridge. Someone had just been shot and he was holding on to a recently fired weapon.

The crush of Vietnamese carrying picket signs shielded him from the view of law enforcement officers rapidly flooding the scene. To his continued surprise, he realized that they were concealing him purposefully with their bodies, with their banners. Protecting him. The way they would someone who'd just rid them of a terrible evil. His back was patted, his free hand pumped, and what few words he could catch had to do with "thank you" and "he deserved it."

Then the rifle was plucked from his unresisting

hand. He found himself staring into the face of an Asian man toting press credentials.

"I'll see this disappears," the journalist was saying. Then they made eye contact and just stared at one another, an odd sort of not-quite-recognition taking them both unawares. McGee didn't know the man, had never seen him or met him or spoken to him before, but something was so familiar. He just couldn't seem to place him in this setting. Those eyes, looking up at him, wanting…something, what was it? The vibration of white noise intensified in his head until it drowned out the sounds around him. He couldn't hear himself ask, "Who are you? How do I know you?"

Then the journalist tucked the rifle beneath the flap of his raincoat and urged, "Go. Hurry," before he slipped away in the panicked throng.

Good idea. He got a very big sense of being in a very wrong place.

As he started to turn, he noticed a striking Vietnamese woman in the crowd circling the fallen figure. He knew her by sight, if not name, just as she seemed to know him. Her features sharpened with shock and then another emotion, one that even at this distance he recognized as hatred. She whirled around, searching for and finally finding her husband as he pushed through the throng of people to get to her side. She grabbed Patrick Kelly's arm and pointed, her gestures and agitated speech telegraphing a mounting hysteria. Then Kelly's gaze followed her directing hand right to where McGee was standing.

And behind Kelly stood a dismayed Barbara D'Angelo, her features frozen in shock.

Regret clear in his expression, Kelly called to the nearest officer, but before the cop could look in his direction, McGee was gone.

She could feel him in the shadows of the room without turning on the lights. As she reached for the switch, he caught her hand to still the motion. His touch was cool compared to her almost feverish state.

"Leave them off," came his quiet command. "Your bags are packed. I've rented a car for you. Don't ask questions. Just go."

The firm push of his orders had her digging in her heels. She would not be chased off without an explanation.

"He was our only lead."

The calm in his tone fractured. "Don't you think I know that?" She heard him take a quick breath then exhale slowly at a modulated pace. "You need to go now while you can still get out of town. It won't take them long to put two and two together and get me and you. You don't want to get caught up in this."

"Did you kill him?"

Silence.

She slipped her hand from his restraining grip. Light flooded the foyer, making her blink and squint against it. His gaze bored into hers, never wavering, as steady as a pale blue laser. No expression registered upon the razor-sharp angles of his face. Her heart beating hard and frantically, she repeated the question.

"Did you kill him?"

She expected a quick denial, anything but the soft-spoken truth he delivered.

"I don't know."

She searched for some shred of emotion in that long beloved face. She could have been looking upon one of the city's many monuments for what little he betrayed.

"What do you mean, you don't know? How could you not know? McGee, how could you not know?"

Finally a flicker behind his eyes. Not furtive, but fearful. "I wasn't actually there at the time."

Too many shades of meaning colored that claim. Her thoughts started spinning in a thousand different directions. But oddly, none of them led away from him in fright.

"We've got to get out of the city."

We. Surprise crumpled the chiseled lines of his face. He stared at her in disbelief and dismay. "There is no *we.* Barbara, you've got to get the hell out of here. This isn't a game any more."

"It was never a game to me."

With that roughly spoken fact, she moved past him into the room, where their bags were already packed for a quick getaway. As if it had been planned. As if he'd been prepared.

But, of course, that was part of his training. To expect the unexpected.

So far, it had all been unexpected where Barbara was concerned.

Think. Think.

Would McGee have pulled the trigger? Frye was Tag's only link to his past. Why would he want him dead?

She drew a slow breath to flush the clutter from her brain. Focus. Think.

She took her room key and laid it on the dresser. Hoisting her bags, she asked, "Where's the car?"

He started to relax his stance, but the tension remained in his expression. A hard, resigned expression. Almost regret. As if he were disappointed that she was taking the out he offered. "I moved it to one of the side streets. A white Buick Le Sabre."

Nice and nondescript. He'd been a busy boy.

"Bring it around to the rear exit. I'll meet you there."

"Barbara."

She didn't turn. She didn't want to see the evidence of the emotion she heard in his voice as he hesitated.

"Go," she prompted. "Hurry!"

She never heard the door close behind him.

Her insides started trembling, a quiet quivering at first and then building to soul-shaking tremors. What was she doing? What was she thinking? He couldn't assure her that he hadn't pulled the trigger.

A quiet calm seeped in, covering doubt, shrouding reason in a dense, blanking fog.

None of it mattered. They were in this together. They had a mutual cause. That goal hadn't changed. And there was no way he was going to skip out on her again, leaving her with all the responsibilities. This time, she meant to see that he kept his promises.

It was shamefully easy.

She toted her wheeled baggage right past the police already swarming the lobby on the way to Frye's room. One of them even held the door open for her. "Have a nice evening, ma'am."

A nice evening, indeed. On the run with a possible killer. She expelled her breath in a shaky gust.

As she pulled the bags toward the curb, a white Buick pulled up, nice and easy, in no hurry at all, its trunk popping. She slung the bags into it and then got into the passenger seat. They slipped away from the hotel without notice.

"Head south," was all Barbara would say, but her thoughts were far ahead, already at their destination.

The drive was uneventful. They avoided the main roads, slipping out of Virginia and into the Carolinas. They were crossing into Florida when Barbara stirred from her fitful napping. The faint grays of dawn etched a harsh lithograph of the man behind the wheel. When she asked him to, he pulled into the next rest stop without question. After a brief stretch, with necessities seen to, she returned to the car.

"I'll drive."

He didn't argue, slipping silently into the shotgun position.

Florida was a long state. It took long hours to traverse the busy interstates leading to Miami. It gave Barbara too much time to think as Tag dozed in the seat beside her.

Had he fired the shot—an assassin's shot—to end Frye's life?

Her heart rebelled against what her mind was considering. Taggert McGee came from a harsh, even brutal past, from a family that had no respect for the law or love for their fellow man. He'd gone from that ugly place to one even crueler, to one that made cold, calculating murderers out of boys like him, Robert and Chet. Robert had come back with a thankfully blanked memory of what he'd done while Chet still reveled in it. What about Tag? Was he still working in tandem with Chet? Had this all been some carefully planned ruse to get her to play accomplice to their scheme?

Her daughter's life and that of her granddaughter could well depend upon how she read the current situation. How rusty those intuitive skills had gotten while living a life of pampered privilege. Could she trust them any more than she could the man beside her?

He's dangerous, Frye had told her. Was he right? Shouldn't he know? After all, Tag was his patient... had been his patient. His experiment. And now that Frye was dead, who had the knowledge to bring him out of the mists concealing his past?

He's dangerous.

She glanced beside her. In the warmth of midday, he appeared all bronzed and relaxed in slumber. Gentler, somehow, without the harsh edges. Like the young man she remembered. The one she still held in her heart. Could that man who'd once discussed poetry and politics in the tall grasses behind the high-school bleachers with her be capable of such a deliberate act of violence? Could the man who shared his DNA with her treasured daughter also be a cold, emotionless killer? Was he the same kind of monster Vietnam had made of Chet Allen?

No. She couldn't have been so wrong about him. Not then. Not now.

He made a soft sound in his sleep and turned toward her on the seat. Without the knife-edge alertness, he looked younger, kinder, blameless. The man who had courted her sweetly, whose stirring kisses coaxed her into surrendering her virginity with little or no objection. And then had left her and the child she was carrying for another to provide for and protect.

What did she really know about the man she'd so briefly loved and eternally pined for? Enough to justify riding across country with him, a jump ahead of the law? Enough to trust him with her safety…her heart?

Agitated and exhausted beyond clear thought, she reached for the radio, hoping for distraction.

"…have an all-points bulletin out for the man suspected in the shooting. McGee, who had been a psychiatric patient of Frye's, is considered armed and dangerous. Anyone with any information…"

She shut the radio off.

Barbara glanced to the right to see a stern-faced Tag McGee straightening in his seat. She couldn't help the sudden jump of alarm that had her stiffening at his movements. But he was only reaching up to rub his eyes.

"Looks like he might get his book deal after all. Or at least a low-end movie of the week."

Barbara said nothing, concentrating on the road. She could feel his study of her and didn't relax until his attention turned to their surroundings.

"Where are we?" he asked, frowning at the sight of palm trees lining the road.

"Just entered Dade County."

"Miami?"

She nodded.

He eyed her with sudden suspicion. "What's in Miami?"

"My parents."

A long pause. Then Tag swore. "Just when I thought things couldn't get any worse."

Chapter 8

The home of a retired judge was probably the last place the law would think to look for a wanted man. And it was the last place Tag McGee would have chosen to hide.

Joseph and Claudia Calvin lived beyond just well. Their eighties-style home of glass and steel sat on the water's edge of South Beach like a modern art sculpture. All precision angles and cold surfaces, it reflected the man McGee remembered. As a teen, he'd been awed by Judge Joe and the sleek Bohemian woman who was Barbara's mother. They represented everything he considered as good, successful and admirable. Everything his own family was not. And they'd both condemned him by circumstance, without giving him a second chance or a second thought.

These were the people Barbara had brought him to for help.

He was a dead man.

Claudia Calvin answered the door. In her mid-seventies, she still looked like a ditzy flower child with her mop top of curls, flowing crinkle skirt and multiple necklaces over a white embroidered tunic. She'd gotten in on the ground floor of modern psychotherapy and pioneered getting in touch with one's feelings to the pre-baby-boomer generation. Her soft, somewhat silly exterior hid the shrewd, razor-sharp mind that dissected with analytical skill. And he could see that clinical brain processing the sight of the two of them together on her front steps.

"Barbara, what a nice surprise. And Mr. McGee, if my memory serves me."

If Barbara was a surprise of a pleasant sort, Tag was certain he was a shock rating right up there with discovering poodle poo on the bottom of her Italian shoes only after she'd crossed a plush pastel carpet. And the feeling was mutual.

"Mrs. Calvin, how good of you to remember."

Her eyes narrowed. Oh, yes. He could see she was remembering everything. Then her gaze darted to the left and right to see if anyone had marked their arrival. She gripped her daughter's arm, firmly commanding, "Come in, dear. There's no need for you to stand out in the hot sun."

Where the neighbors might see them and recognize them as the fugitives on the news.

They stepped into a sea of pale turquoise and rose

tranquility right out of an art deco *Miami Vice* episode—white furniture, white walls and white stone with tasteful splashes of the muted colors in the appropriate places. Obviously done by a highly paid interior designer because there wasn't one hint of warmth, personality or intimacy in the place.

Rather like the Calvins, in that regard.

"What's that son of a bitch doing in my house?"

Retirement had done nothing to soften Judge Joe Calvin, nor had time mellowed his opinion of the man his daughter once wanted to date.

"I see you remember me, too." No smile accompanied that mild remark, nor did Tag extend his hand to offer a truce. Not just to have it bitten off. "You haven't changed a bit, sir." Still the same unpleasant, narrow-minded bastard he'd been thirty years ago.

And Barbara was still Daddy's little girl.

She stepped between them and into her father's reluctant embrace.

"We need your help or we wouldn't be here."

"You shouldn't be here at all. Not with him," the judge growled. His glare over the top of his daughter's head was eviscerating. "It's on the news. What the hell have you gotten yourself into, Barbara? Didn't I always tell you he was no good?"

"Judge, please," she begged so miserably the old man relented enough to pat her on the back.

"Would anyone like coffee? I just put some on. Let's sit down. There's no reason we can't have a conversation like reasonable adults."

Smooth, cool and condescending. Claudia was the

perfect manipulator. De-escalate the tension first, then go right for the throat.

"I don't want him here," Calvin snarled.

"No more than I want to be here, sir."

The two men locked stares. McGee was no longer a young man easily reduced by the distaste of his elders. He'd been in a war. He'd killed for his country. And he'd be damned if he was going to back down before the other's rudeness and hostility. But it was the man's house. And he was past the front door, farther than he'd gotten the first time.

Ordinarily he would have just walked away. However, Barbara was looking up at him through beseeching eyes and even if he didn't owe the old bigot an ounce of respect, he did value her feelings enough to stay, as he should have so many years ago.

"Right this way," Claudia urged with the sincerity of a tour guide at a popular attraction. She led them into the sunken living room with its breathtaking ocean view. The judge went to stand at the stone fireplace, while his wife poured from an imported porcelain service.

Tag sat uneasily on one of the white cushioned bamboo sofas and was surprised when Barbara settled at his side. She didn't sit close enough to actually touch him but the link of proximity was unmistakable.

Judge Calvin's brow lowered like hurricane clouds. "So, what do you expect me to do, Barbara? I'm not on the bench any more so I don't have any legal pull to get your friend here out of whatever trouble he's made for himself."

"I wouldn't expect you to try, Judge." Was there just

a pinch of resentment in that calm statement of fact? Barbara shifted her focus to her other parent. "Actually, I'm here for Mother's help."

She went on to lay out the events of the past few days with all the detachment of someone describing an interesting case study rather than a situation that directly affected their futures. Barbara knew her parents would react half as well to an emotional appeal as they would an impersonal puzzle.

"What do you know about the use of hypnosis in the military, Mother?"

Claudia gave a delicate shrug. "I know various levels of mind control were tested during the Korean conflict and, of course, in Vietnam, using hypnosis with and without the reenforcement of narcotics. I'm not talking about *Manchurian Candidate*-type control, but just minor tampering with the human psyche in hopes of gaining positive results."

"Like psychotic behavior? Paranoia? Memory loss? To turn a soldier into a killer? Just how is that seen as positive?"

Claudia exhibited no visual response to Tag's cool attack on her profession. "These things don't manifest themselves without an underlying weakness in the subject. Hypnosis is still just suggestion. It can't force a man a behave contrary to his nature. It would only sharpen those attributes in his personality."

"To erase the conscience in a criminal mind," Calvin interjected. His steely stare never left McGee.

"Or," Barbara extrapolated from a different side of the spectrum, "if you have a decent man with high moral character and you insert the idea that what they're to do is right and justified, then they would not think they were doing wrong. Isn't that the way it works, Mother?"

"Theoretically, yes. All hypothetically speaking. And, of course, it would depend upon the susceptibility of the subject involved, of how open they are to taking subconscious suggestion."

"And if drugs were used, that would lower that vulnerability?"

As she spoke in a detached tone, Tag felt Barbara's knuckles graze his thigh. It might have been by accident. Then her fingers spread over the top of his hand to curl and hold tight to create a united, if silent, front. A gesture not missed by either parent. Tag was careful not to respond beneath their microscopic glares but inwardly, his pulse kicked into high gear at the gentle press of support.

"This really isn't my area, Barbara," Claudia protested modestly. "I practiced regression therapy working with troubled children, not traumatized adults."

"But the mind still works the same way."

"Within different ranges of experience and personality development, yes. What is it you want me to do, Barbara? Psychoanalyze your friend?" She said the word *friend* as if it implied the most unsavory and unacceptable traits imaginable.

"No. I want you to hypnotize him. I want you to try to unlock what he can't remember."

Protest came instantaneously from all three corners. "Nonsense."

"That's not possible."

"No way."

Barbara was adamant. "There is no other way," she said to McGee. "Frye is dead. Whatever he put in or took out of your memory is out of reach. Don't you see? We have to get into those secrets Chet was warning of and Frye was trying to bury. Don't you want to know what he did?"

Tag stared at her, numb and horrified all at once because suddenly he wasn't sure he did want to know. How could he handle finding out that he was just like Chet? That he'd been a tool of indiscriminate murder? That, perhaps to keep his fractured personality safe, he'd killed the one man who could expose him?

Hadn't he been hiding from the truth all these years? Tunneling into the quiet forest where there'd be no triggers of memory, no reason to wonder, no need to find out just what kind of man Frye had turned him into?

The kind of man Barbara D'Angelo would regard with fear and loathing.

Then her fingers squeezed ever so lightly about his.

What good would he ever be to this woman if he, again, abandoned her because of his own weaknesses?

"If you think it might help."

"Barbara, hypnosis isn't an exact science under the most ideal control circumstances, and what you're asking is hardly ideal."

Barbara looked to her mother. "Are you saying you won't try? To save a man's life? My life and Tessa's?"

"I think we should just call the police," Calvin muttered.

But Claudia was already fingering one of the baubles she wore around her neck and studying Tag as if he were some new species she'd be able to slap her name and reputation on in some professional journal.

"If experimental drugs were used, I might not be able to do any good," she was saying more to herself than them. "I suppose I could start with a simple regression technique and go from there."

"Claudia, you're making us accomplices here. Hypnosis isn't admissible in court."

She barely acknowledged her husband. "My office is quiet and the light is muted. Mr. McGee, come this way."

Following Claudia Calvin was one of the hardest things he could ever remember doing. But not so hard as leaving her daughter behind three decades ago. The thought of giving this coolly clinical woman any power over him sat uneasily in his soul. That she would be stripping his mind to its most vulnerable state and tampering where she had no right to be made him break into a sweat. Then he considered the courage and faith of Barbara D'Angelo hopping into that Buick with him, trusting that he wasn't everything the news portrayed him to be, and his fear diminished.

Maybe just a peek inside wouldn't do any harm….

Claudia took him into a claustrophobic little room lined with books and oriental knickknacks. The scent of green tea, candles and incense brought an instant ache to his temples. The room was furnished with a desk on the point of collapse beneath a weight of papers, several beanbag-type chairs and a squishy leather sofa. Framed certificates vied for wall space next to inspirational posters. Chaos and calm.

"On the couch, I suppose?"

"Wherever you're comfortable."

Isle Royale came to mind. Cautiously, he settled into one of the beanbag chairs and was immediately enveloped by its loose contours. Smiling at his choice, Claudia angled a second chair so they were face-to-face. They regarded each other for a long moment.

"Don't you trust me, Mr. McGee?"

"No."

His honesty made her smile again, more naturally this time. "Then the feeling's mutual. Let's go treasure hunting, shall we? How did you start your sessions with your other doctor?"

"He usually took me dancing and bought dinner."

Her laugh was surprisingly warm, gentle. Like her daughter's. Tag relaxed a notch and took a deep breath.

"Good." Claudia removed one of her necklaces. Its pendant was made of prismed glass, shooting out dazzling color with every turn or twist. "I want you to continue to breathe deep, let your shoulders slump, let your arms, your hands get heavy, heavier, too heavy to lift. Watch the glass and try not to focus on anything but the light. You can hear my voice and you can respond to my questions, but everything else is very, very far away. Let your thoughts empty. Let them drain away like the sands in an hourglass. Watch the sand trickle down. The weight of the sand is pulling your eye lids down, down, down. Now, you can only hear my voice. Can you hear me?"

"Yes."

"Can you tell me your name?"

"Taggert McGee."

"And can you tell me where you are?"

"The last place I want to be."

Again the soft chuckle. The sound moved over and around his thoughts where they rested peacefully in the dark haven she'd made for him. His body seemed disconnected from those lazy ruminations. Until her next suggestion.

"I want you to go back with me just in your mind, back to a place not as peaceful as this one, to another country, another time. It's the early seventies. Can you tell me what you see?"

He sucked in a sudden breath and all his muscles stiffened. Again, her voice was a soothing balm.

"Nothing you see can hurt you. You're just watching. Like television. What are you watching?"

"Chet."

"Where are you?"

"Sniper school. He's got cigarette butts in his ears for ear plugs. We were there for four weeks, practicing every day. Chet could shoot the balls off a mosquito with the Redfield. I liked the Starlight. Sometimes I'd dream in the shades of green and black I saw through that scope."

"How did you feel about what you did?"

"Feel?"

"Pride? Satisfaction? Pleasure?"

"I didn't feel anything. It was against the rules."

"And you always played by the rules?"

"Yes, ma'am."

"Whose rules, Sergeant McGee? Who made those rules?"

His breathing hitched and began to hurry. His head rolled back and forth against the back of the chair in sudden agitation. "I don't know. I can't see them. I don't know. I can only hear what they tell me to do."

"What do they tell you?"

"I don't remember. I'm not supposed to remember."

"Today you can. Today it's alright to remember."

And he could hear his own voice describing the horror that had been Vietnam as if he were doing a feature on the Travel Channel. The pictures were so clear, so real, yet part of someone else's impressions. He'd never been to the places he described, had never done the things he started to name. Villages, cities, sometimes with Chet Allen, sometimes with Robert D'Angelo, sometimes alone, so alone. The feeling of isolation crept up from the soles of his feet, freezing like ice water, like death, until he was struggling against it.

He couldn't hear the words she was speaking even though he was aware of the sound of her voice droning behind the sudden hard and loud pounding in his head. His heartbeats.

Then another sound. Weeping. Awful, anguished weeping. A woman wailing, begging, pleading for the lives of her family. He recoiled from the image, denying it, refusing to acknowledge it.

But the sound of those heartrending sobs drew him back, forcing him to leave the safety of detached observer to step into that ugly scene. To confront the demons from his dreams.

His eyes snapped open and he could see her face, the woman who'd been with Patrick Kelly. There was blood on the floor. He could smell its thick, metallic odor. There was blood on his boots.

He stepped back and her hands kept reaching for him, beseeching, grasping. He felt her touch on his knee, so real and warm and firm and the shock of it zapped through him like an electric current. Panic, horror, dismay surged up, drowning him in sensation.

He had to get away. He started to retreat, physically, mentally, and that's when he heard it. The two words crisply spoken as if the speaker were kneeling beside him.

Kingdom come.

And everything went dark, like a light switching off inside his head.

Then Claudia Calvin's soft, intense instruction.

"Listen to me. Hear only my voice. You're leaving that time, that place behind. As you come back toward the sound of my voice, you'll bring those things you saw with you but they won't be able to harm you. Just like a movie that you've been watching. Not real. Not able to touch you. Bring them back with you. Back to the sound of my voice. Where are you now, Mr. McGee?"

"Miami."

"Good. Just a few more questions. Did you kill Dr. Frye?"

"No."

A moment's pause. "Tell me what you do remember."

"That's against the rules."

"What were you thinking, bringing him here?"

Faced with her father's disapproving anger, Barbara felt like a little child again, the one who cringed beneath his censure, the one who tried desperately to win his approval. Doubts and insecurities scratched their way back to the surface. *A proper young lady doesn't argue with her elders. You disappoint me, Barbara, me and your mother. What an ungrateful child you've become. You should be ashamed.*

And she was. How could she bring distress to these two individuals who had sacrificed so much for her? She was ungrateful. She was selfish. She was thinking of only her own needs. A humbling apology was already shaping on her lips when she stopped herself cold in sudden recognition.

She saw Tessa in the slump of her own shoulders, in the meek lowering of her eyes, in the hollow shrinking of her self-esteem. She was reminded of her own daughter suffering similarly through her growing-up years, struggling to earn affection from a man who was a father in name only. A man who withheld approval and suppressed the spirit as a means of control.

The repetition of that demeaning pattern was a wake-up slap. Her posture straightened, her tone cooled.

"I thought you might love me enough to want to help me. Was I wrong?"

Joseph Calvin sighed in aggravation, annoyed that she'd play the emotion card to trump him. "This has nothing to do with you. It's that boy."

"He's not a boy, Judge. He hasn't been that boy for a long time."

"And what kind of man has he become? Someone who would drag you into danger like…"

"Like Robert did?"

"That was different," he blustered. "Robert was a victim. He was innocent."

"And Tag isn't? Why would you assume that? Just because of who his family was? Where's the fairness in that?"

That got the reaction she'd hoped for. A man who prided himself on being impartial, he recoiled from her suggestion that he'd been anything but. Before he could make a statement in his own defense, she continued, recklessly, to pursue her case.

"You were wrong to pronounce sentence on him without any proof. You never even took the time to get to know him. You saw only what you wanted to see. And you were wrong. I loved him, Daddy. I loved him more than my very life."

The judge reared back with shock and dismay. And ultimately disgust. "You were just a child. You didn't know what was best."

"And you did? You thought it would be better for me to spend thirty loveless years with Robert D'Angelo rather than take a chance on finding happiness with someone whose pedigree didn't match your expectations? Robert was your choice and you made sure he was the only one left to me. You couldn't have made your wishes any clearer if you'd held a shotgun to our heads. It wasn't about what was best for me. It was about what was best for you and your image."

"Robert was a good provider for you and your children. You can't deny that."

"And I don't. Robert gave us everything we needed or wanted. Things, Dad. He gave us things."

He snorted. "Don't tell me. You would have rather lived on love. Barbara, you're fifty years old and I still have to tell you to grow up."

"I am grown up, Dad. And I've grown old and alone, and I've missed my only chance to be truly happy."

"Since when is it a crime to want the best for your child? That McGee boy couldn't give it to you. All he could give you was heartache. Do you think you fooled us, sneaking out to meet with him? He made you into a liar, Barbara, to cover up what you knew was wrong for you."

"Wrong for you, Dad. You pushed us into doing what we had to do to see one another. You wouldn't let us have a decent relationship. You wouldn't give us a chance."

He began to pace, building up his argument the way the trial lawyers used to do before his bench. "You were a child, Barbara. He was bringing you down to his level with the lies, with the secrets. Using Robert shamelessly so we would think you were safely dating him instead of someone we didn't approve of. How do you think it made me feel to learn my daughter was using others to cover for the nights she spent doing God knows what? To find out that she'd gotten a post office box to carry on correspondence behind our back? If you weren't ashamed of him, why would you go to such lengths?"

"Who told you about those things?" Barbara gasped.

"One of your girlfriends who was a true friend. One who didn't want to see you getting into trouble. I don't remember her name."

Barbara's question was a whisper. "What did you do, Daddy?"

He flushed, looking uncomfortable. "I had the mail redirected from the box. You were a minor—"

"You had no right!" Then, in a breathless voice, she asked, "He sent letters?"

"At first."

"Where are they?" Her heart was beating hard and fast in anticipation. Then he cruelly cut through her hopes.

"I burned them. He was no good for you, Barbara. It was an infatuation. I don't apologize for what I did. You weren't thinking clearly. I knew Robert would take responsibility for you, the way he did for his baby."

"Tessa isn't Robert's child, Dad."

Silence. A thunderous, intense silence as Joseph Calvin absorbed the truth. Then he hissed, "And you let Robert think—"

"Robert knew. And he knew you would never accept a child of Tag's. We both knew that you never would have let me keep the baby. So he offered me a way out, the only way you left for me to take that wouldn't embarrass you and our family name. Robert understood how important that was. It was a sacrifice I was willing to make for Tessa."

Calvin huffed and puffed, irate. "And McGee just turned his back and you and the child."

"Tessa, Dad. She has a name. And no. He never knew. He still doesn't know."

Calvin might have felt vindicated if she told him that she'd thought just as little of Tag's inherent decency. She'd also believed Tag had abandoned her and the child they made without a word, without a care. But she wouldn't let her father off the hook any more than she could excuse her own failings. That would be her guilty secret, and it burned in her breast with a hot, heavy shame.

"And Tessa? Does she know?"

"Now. But not until after Robert died."

"What a mess you've made of everything, Barbara."

His resigned sigh of condemnation defined everything about their relationship. She saw that, finally. She would never win his love or approval, just as Tessa had struggled in vain to claim Robert's. She had made a mess by trying to please the wrong people. But perhaps it wasn't too late to clean it up.

Her mother and McGee returned to the room. Their expressions offered no reason for optimism.

"I'm sorry, Barbara," Claudia said. "Whatever safeguards that doctor placed, they go much deeper than I thought. He wasn't able to bring back the things he began to recall while he was under. I made some notes but they don't seem to mean anything to him now. I know one thing. This isn't PTSD. It's hypnosis-induced amnesia covered by a very precise trail of false memories. The truth is there. He just can't get to it. I couldn't even scratch the surface."

Disappointment on top all else brought frustrated tears to her eyes. She'd hoped… Barbara blinked determinedly. Her attention focused on Tag.

"You couldn't remember anything?" she prompted gently.

"Nothing of any value. This was a waste of time." He was again all curt, controlled energy. And whatever he was feeling was suppressed behind his immobile expression. He was a stranger again, not the man who'd asked so poignantly for her to help him hold on to the memories they'd made between them. He nodded to her parents. "I'm sorry for the intrusion. I'll be on my way before you're linked to my problems."

And he started toward the front door, walking right by her without a glance.

Barbara hesitated only an instant. Then she embraced her mother, pressing a quick kiss on her unlined cheek and murmuring, "Thank you for trying." Then she exchanged a long unapologetic stare with her father before saying, "Goodbye."

As she turned, Calvin called, "You're making a serious mistake, Barbara."

She paused but didn't turn. "I've made them before. But this isn't one of them."

And she ran after the man she loved.

Chapter 9

When she opened the passenger side door, Barbara was greeted by a brief flicker of surprise and then the continued cool Tag had carried from inside the house.

"Get out, Barbara."

"No." She buckled the seat belt about her in a defiant gesture. He didn't start the car. Nor did he look at her again as he spoke in that same flat tone.

"Stay here," he insisted. "They'll make sure you're safe. You belong here, not on the run with me."

"I'm where I belong right now. Let's go."

Still no turn of the key. Instead, he tugged on a ball cap, pulling it down low, and used dark glasses to shield his identity from the last of the day's sun.

"Your folks are probably on the phone to the police.

How long before they catch up to us? I don't want you with me when that happens."

"They won't catch you."

"They will if I have to drag you along. You'll slow me down. I don't have time to babysit a pampered society girl who can't be trusted to be strong when the going gets tough."

That took her right to the heart. For a moment, she couldn't get over the pain of it, but she did. She'd put aside his hurtful words for when she had time to let her spirit bleed over them.

"Look who's talking about trust. Who's failed whom, McGee? I'm just protecting my interests. So start the damned car."

Her gritty demand had the desired effect. He pulled away from the curb with a jolt as harsh as the one that wrung her emotions. She gripped the door handle and pursed her lips together even tighter.

The truth was, she had failed him under pressure. She hadn't believed in their love, a love that still tormented her with those tantalizing what-ifs.

So she stayed silent and let him drive, not asking questions, not trying to find a chink in the impenetrable wall that had slammed back down around him.

She stopped watching the road signs through eyes too tired and tear-drenched to focus and simply leaned back and eased them shut. It didn't matter where they were going when the road wasn't carrying them to the answers they needed to find.

She wondered what her daughter was doing. Was Tessa still blissfully ignorant of the danger she was in?

Or had Allen decided to step up his intimidation? How far could she trust him to keep his word, to follow the time schedule he'd given them?

A heavy, desperate ache built around her heart, pressing, crushing, as she mourned the loss of family.

She was on run with an intimate stranger, placing herself in deeper peril by the mile. To what purpose?

She should have gone to the authorities in the first place. She should have stepped back and accepted the fact that she was what Tag accused her of being, what Robert and her parents had always groomed her to be. A pretty piece of useless fluff. A decoration without real utility. Tag was right. She was just getting in his way.

She must have made some unwitting sound of despair for him to reach out to her. His fingertips grazed her damp cheek before tunneling back into her hair. With a touch both gentle and firm in its support, he palmed the back of her head and drew it to his shoulder. She burrowed there, gratefully, emotions too shattered to sustain her in her exhausted state. Silent tears fell. He didn't speak, didn't offer any words of comfort, but none were needed. Just the weight of his hand, the solid curl of his arm, the steady rock of his breathing was enough as he continued to drive into fast-approaching darkness.

"Barb, wake up. We're here."

Groggily, she leaned away from him, unaware of exactly when she'd fallen asleep. She glanced around. "Where's here?"

"The best I could afford with the cash on hand. Sorry."

The term Roach Motel came to mind as she exited the car where they'd parked next to a particularly odorous Dumpster. One dim, flickering light illuminated the broken walk leading along the back of the single-story building. She was glad for what the shadows concealed. Between the battered pickup trucks and abandoned trash bags, the surroundings didn't warrant a closer look. She picked her way over a pool of broken glass and wad of fast-food wrappers to join Tag at the door to their overnight accommodations. He'd set his jaw against the need for further apology as he turned the key and switched on the single light.

It was spartan, only a double bed covered by a faded green spread flanked by a rickety nightstand and a two-drawer pressed wood dresser. No television, no chair, no amenities of any kind. It was old but clean. There was a thin door leading the way to a bathroom and tiny shower; for the moment, those were the only luxuries she required.

"What do you need from the car?"

"Just my overnight case. Do you need the bathroom before I hit the shower?"

"No. Go ahead."

Such personal talk for two distant traveling companions.

She shut herself in where the cracked tiles were held together in a sort of low-rent mosaic by age-stained grout and waited for the much anticipated hot water. At least the pressure was good, she thought with a sigh as she stepped beneath the spray. The plastic curtain fluttered as the bathroom door opened. She froze, pushing her hair out of her eyes, wondering wildly, with a sudden surprising rush of nervous excitement, if Tag meant to join her.

"I thought you might like these."

Her bag of bath necessities nudged beyond the edge of the curtain, her scented shampoo, bath gels and milled soap looking glaringly out of place in the seedy surroundings.

"Thanks."

The soft sound of the door closed on her fantasies. What had she expected?

Just because the idea of sex with Tag McGee had percolated beneath the surface of her more rational emotions from the moment she'd lost herself looking up into his clear blue eyes didn't mean the same had occurred to him. He hadn't said specifically that there wasn't a Mrs. McGee or a soon-to-be Mrs. McGee in the picture somewhere. She'd assumed that just because the memory of what they'd shared still created an enticing friction at every sensory nerve ending, he'd be similarly chafing to find out if it would be just as good—no, just as spectacular—as it had been that first time around.

She wanted to know. She wanted to know so bad, her knees had been shaking when he'd opened the bathroom door. If he'd chosen to look behind Curtain Number One, he would have found her lathered and ready before even wetting the soap.

Maybe it was the adrenaline rush, the forced proximity, the threat of danger that had all her senses tingling. Or maybe it was the simple fact that no man but him had ever stirred her to such a frenzy of need. Not as a teen. Not as a grown woman. She'd longed for him, for the chance to return to his arms, to suck up his kisses, to glory in his lovemaking until the reality of him in the next room, available and sexy as hell, was enough to have her breathing heavily. Even if it was just for one night, one time, one more memory, it would be enough to sustain her. Even a spiny cactus required the occasional watering. And she'd never felt so parched in her entire life.

She lathered and scrubbed and massaged a citrus scent into her skin before toweling dry and turbaning the thin terry about her damp hair. Putting on the stale clothes she'd worn for two days was out of the question. Planning to ask Tag to retrieve her other bag, she swaddled herself in the other good-sized bath sheet and stepped out into the dark room. McGee stood silhouetted at the window, peering through the inch-wide gap he'd left in the limp curtains. He was in jeans and a T-shirt. The dark fabric stretched taut across his shoulders. Hard muscled arms pushed from the short sleeves. He was coiled and ready for anything. And so was she. He didn't turn.

"Feel better?"

"Than what?"

He did look her way then, a slight smile etched upon ragged features. A smile that froze and thinned with strain as his no-longer-cool gaze took in the sight of her bared shoulders and shapely legs.

Then it hit him, hard, the fact of the two of them

alone in a no-tell motel room with one bed and thirty years of pent-up wanting. He tried to speak, but his tongue seemed to stick to the roof of his mouth, probably seared by the same sudden blaze of heat that pooled liquid lava low below his belt.

She appeared to have something to say, but apparently the same abrupt loss of oral command struck her, too. She stared back, mesmerized by the intensity of desire she read in every stark line of his face, in the unmistakable ridge building behind the zipper of his snug jeans.

It wasn't alarm or anything like it reflected back in the soft wetting of her lips. So he took a chance, forcing words through the Sahara-dry passage of his throat.

"How is it that you can still believe in me enough to be here when I can't even trust myself?"

A determined swallow worked her creamy neck, but her gaze never wavered. "It's in your eyes."

"What is?"

"What I've always seen there. The promise of everything I could ever need or want."

He processed that claim slowly, denying his mind's quick rejection, as well as his heart's all-too-eager acceptance. There was too much history to take that answer at face value.

"Why wasn't it enough, Barb?" he needed to know.

"It wasn't for an insecure seventeen-year-old. I never heard from you, Tag. My father intercepted your letters. I never saw them. I never knew until now that you wrote me. And it broke my heart. But I'm not that little girl anymore. I don't need those same guarantees now. And what I want, at the moment, is a lot less complex."

He started to shake his head in deference to the complications she so conveniently overlooked. But then she ended their disagreement with a conclusive, if unfair, action.

The towel dropped.

Before him stood the youthful perfection that had driven his postadolescent hormones crazy, softened yet strengthened by the years and three children. He hadn't been a monk for the last thirty years, but at the moment he couldn't remember the details of any other female form.

"Pretty sneaky way to defuse an argument," he managed to say.

Without a hint of girlish shyness, Barbara Calvin D'Angelo merely smiled. "Old age and treachery overcoming youth and skill."

He couldn't get beyond the sudden sensual stupor to cross the room. His delay brought a beguiling blush of uncertainty up Barbara's gloriously naked chest and neck to warm her cheeks. Her next suggestion was no less direct but slightly more imploring.

"Since you passed on what was behind Curtain Number One, you can have what's under Sheet Number Two. If you want to."

"Deal of the century," he concluded.

She'd stripped back the bedspread by the time he reached her. He stilled further movement by cupping her chin in one hand. As she looked up at him through eyes luminescent with yearning, he tugged the towel from her tousled hair so he could lean into her, nudging those fragrant strands until his senses filled with the fresh scent of her. How he had dreamed of this moment only to have those imaginings fall so far short of the actual paradise of having her offered so sweetly, so completely.

"I have thought of little else for longer than I can remember," he murmured into her ear.

Her lips grazed his throat. "Don't think. Do."

He scooped her up, holding her tight, savoring the feel of her all sleek and curvy against him. Turning, he arranged her malleable form upon the starched white sheet. She gleamed there, a pearl of unequaled value. When he paused to remove his own clothes, she pulled him down to her, so that he fell across her, scuffing her tender breasts with the rough fabric of his shirt. Then he forgot about everything beyond the warm pleasures of her kiss.

Hot, hungry, urgently seeking, her mouth worked against his, demanding, pleading, pleasing in ways that short-circuited rational thought. He didn't think. He just reacted to this unexpected second chance at his heart's every desire.

She tasted like a young man's hopes and a grown man's fantasies. Warm, sweet, willing. He learned her contours all over again, finding them fuller and more satisfying, a finely aged wine appreciated by a true connoisseur. He sipped from the bouquet of her lips, teased his palate with the smoothness of her arched throat, rolled his tongue about the full-bodied bud of her nipples until he was intoxicated. Barbara D'Angelo at any age was a good year. A great year.

He slowed the need to gulp her down with a greedy

desperation because the gradual sampling was far more filling. And rewarding. He returned to dip into the silky cavern of her mouth. She moaned in welcome. He traced her shape with the flat of his hand, smoothing her like a virgin canvas with that claiming pass. Over the swell of her breast, along the curve of her ribs, over the slight mound of her belly while she quivered inch by awakening inch. Her excited breaths brushed in hurried little gusts against his face as he lifted slightly away to watch the evolving pleasure in her expression. Her lashes fluttered wildly as his fingertips stroked up one sleek inner thigh, moving with unerring purpose toward the center of all her passions. Finding her hot, wet, ready for the entry of one finger, two. The walls of her body clutched tight about him, grabbing at the wonderful friction he incited the same way her hands fisted in the sheets.

"McGee, I'm on fire," she cried with a husky urgency that got his own blood hammering hard and fast and furious.

"Burn, baby," he whispered against her panting mouth, "burn."

A sudden tension pulled her every muscle taut and trembling. She quivered there at that seeking pinnacle for a long, expectant second before shuddering, crying out, dissolving into a series of delightful tremors that amazed and inspired him.

For a moment, he was afraid to touch her, wary of stirring her from the languorous state of fulfillment to pursue the increasing necessity of his own release. She was so beautiful, so suddenly fragile with the sheen of satisfaction on her skin, her breaths faint and fast, her features dreamily soft. Then her eyes opened and she looked up at him with the offer of heaven and hell reflecting deep in those emotion-drenched depths. He feared to move lest he break that spell of contentment he saw glowing in her face.

Then she reached up to touch his cheek.

"Oh, McGee, I've missed this. I've missed you."

Could he deny he felt the same?

She guided him back down to the delicious part of her lips, where her tongue lolled about his with a languid sensuality, sucking, swirling his senses into a frenzied state of near madness as she pulled his shirt free from the waistband of his jeans. Her palms pushed the fabric up under his armpits so she could explore the rippled firmness of his abs. Better than she remembered.

While sanity still had a hold on him, he murmured with regret, "I don't have any protection with me, Barb." He hadn't thought…hadn't dared hope… He remembered passing a gas station a block up. He could make a quick dash—

She smoothed his slight frown with the stroke of her forefinger. "Don't worry. I'm out of the reproduction business."

"Oh."

Had it been that long? A sudden, bittersweet remorse came with burying one cherished dream. Having children with Barbara.

Because of his hesitation, she asked, "Are there any other issues we need to concern ourselves with?"

He shook his head, then slowly lowered back onto her tender lips.

She'd been with two men in her life. She'd shared her adulthood and a bed with Robert D'Angelo for thirty years and she'd accepted that both those things would never hold the magical excitement she'd discovered with Taggert McGee. Perhaps because he'd been her first and she was remembering what they'd had through the fanciful impressions of youth. Or so she'd thought until she'd come alive at his reacquainting touch. Tag McGee was, and remained, her one great passion, and now that she'd experienced it again, selfishly, greedily, she didn't want to let go. Not now. Other worries, other fears could wait while she enjoyed this one respite. For this moment, it was about her wants, her needs, her desires.

As a young man, he'd been all sinew and grace. She'd marveled at the sight, at the feel of his hard body. She was no less amazed by what she rediscovered. What he'd gained in body mass had converted quite enticingly into muscle, swells and hollows that she traced in eager exploration as she peeled off his T-shirt. As he leaned back to pull free of the sleeves, she noticed the wink of precious metal against the smooth plane of his chest. Her own seized up with emotion when she recognized the medallion.

He'd kept it. He still wore it.

An aphrodisiac to her thirsting soul.

His clothing tossed carelessly to the floor, he returned to her. The heat and friction of flesh on flesh. Indescribable. Everywhere he touched her, she throbbed and burned. Unbearable. He didn't speak. His touch did the talking. Telling her she was desirable, how much he wanted her, needed this connection as much as she did. Everything she had to hear without saying a word. His hands, his mouth on her breasts, his weight, his hardness upon her body. So familiar and yet so exhilaratingly new. He was, yet he wasn't, the lover she held so close in her memory. The taste, the scent, the feel, all the same. The emotions were different, matured by time, ripened by neglect, ready to explode with the slightest attention.

He seated himself deep inside her and she went off like a Fourth of July extravaganza. Big, shattering, sky-filling bursts followed by the pops and sparks of low-to-the-ground dazzlers. Her body oohed and aahed in spirit-quaking pleasure. Still, his movements provoked her senses to even greater heights, something about rockets' glare and bombs in midair and just as she was sure she could reach that star-spangled high note, his climax carried her with him for a dramatic crescendo.

And then there was silence. Just the sounds of their breathing and the thunder of heartbeats. So beautiful, she wept.

He held her then, gathered close against him, her head on his shoulder, her sated body draped along the length of his with all the animation of the abandoned towel from her hair. Gloriously replete. Thoroughly satisfied. And completely content as she shut her eyes to fall unwittingly to sleep.

* * *

Though his physical self was reading Empty on the energy meter, Tag's mind continued to work, evading rest and the healing happiness Barbara enjoyed.

He still loved her. That was no great surprise. That hadn't changed. Neither had the unpleasant fact that he hadn't been then, and wasn't now, good enough to claim her devotion. This blissful moment, this stolen idyll in a lousy hotel room on the run from the law was all he could have of her.

What he could give her in return held the far greater value. Her safety. He had to make that his priority. It no longer mattered that she'd chosen Robert's security over his affection. That bitter truth had finally burned itself out. They weren't those same kids any more. What mattered was keeping her alive, just as his goal in Vietnam had been protecting his friend so Rob could return to her and see to her happiness in a way he couldn't. His own wants weren't in the equation.

He held her, savoring the feel of her, the softness, the heat, the joy of her total trust and surrender, knowing he had no right to any of it. Her trust was unwarranted. He had no proof that he wasn't everything Frye said. And perhaps more.

When he closed his eyes, he saw bodies of those he'd killed. Not in warfare, not in the jungle. But in hotel rooms like this one, in office suites, in diplomatic cars. Victims he couldn't remember being ordered to take out. Victims who cried out, as Patrick Kelly's wife had done, in blameless terror. He'd lied to Claudia Calvin when he said he had no recall at all after her attempt to unlock his mind. She'd managed to rip a small corner in his psyche and the horror it held just kept trickling out.

What the hell had Frye turned him into?

And now, who was trying to hide what the doctor had done?

The ache in his temples began, a dull, prodding throb. Tension knotted in his belly, building to a pain that rivaled the pleasure Barbara had just given him. Symptoms of a guilt even Claudia Calvin's hypnotic voice couldn't release. Because it would be too much for his soul to bear. He had to know how much more there was behind the void Frye placed in his head and the only one who could tell him now was Chet Allen.

Dawn slipped in quietly and with equal softness, he woke Barbara with a kiss. She murmured sleepily as her eyes opened. Recognition came with a happiness so pure and simple it crushed his heart like an aluminum can.

"I've called a cab to take you back to your parents. Where I'm going, you can't follow."

She was awake then, fully and full of objection. "You can't just run away. What about my daughter? You promised to keep her safe."

Was that it? Was that what was behind her sweet compliance? It wasn't love or even the memory of it that brought Barbara into his arms. It was, as it always had been, her blind devotion to her family above all else. The family that took everything she had to give, leaving nothing left for him.

Fine.

He was off the bed, already dressed in his rumpled clothes.

"I'll keep my promise, Barb. Don't worry. Before I clear my name, I'll play Chet's game and make sure your daughter is safe."

Our daughter, she was about to protest. But the cold set of his features, of his tone, caught her off guard, leaving her mentally scrambling from the luxurious contentment she'd found in his arms. What was going on? Why was he so angry? So anxious to get away?

Before she could grab her own clothes from her opened bag to confront him with what remaining dignity she could salvage, he was gone.

She heard the roar of the motor outside their room and knew there was no use in running after him to plead her case. Or confess her sins. Those would have to wait. For what she'd discovered upon waking was a truth much more galvanizing. Knowledge that the pain of perhaps losing him again was almost as agonizing as it had been half a lifetime ago.

She glanced at her left hand where a simple circle of gold remained to remind her of the empty life she'd been bound to. Slowly, meaningfully, she slipped it free of her finger and set it on the nightstand.

Taggert McGee wasn't walking out on her a second time, not without knowing another truth she'd held on to too long.

A truth that might drive a wedge between them forever.

Chapter 10

He followed her after she and her daughter left the others in their school parking lot and headed north in their SUV. He tracked her down using the numbers in the memory of Barbara's cell phone. She was cautious, so he had to be extra careful to maintain his distance. Someone had trained her well.

The compound she entered provided another degree of difficulty. The security system was state-of-the-art and he was a bit out of practice. Still, he had breached the perimeter without setting off any of the various alarms and had established himself on a high point of ground to observe without contact.

He would have known her by the blond hair. Barbara's daughter. An unidentifiable ache crowded his throat as he watched her move around the vehicle to the passenger door. A preteen girl hopped out. The grand-daughter. He couldn't tell much. He didn't have the proper surveillance equipment. But then he'd planned to get up close and personal, not use intel from afar.

Before the two of them had reached the porch of the truly impressive main house, a man met them, scooping them up with an unabashed affection. The son-in-law. Ex-military. No mistaking the way he moved as he swept the surroundings before leading them to up to the house. They went inside.

He had to get closer to find the best point of entry. It was easy to follow their movements through the huge walls of glass. They weren't expecting to be observed. He waited in the deepest part of the night until they had put the little girl to bed. No need to involve her.

He moved on the house, quick, silent, purposeful. He was across a side porch and inside in a heartbeat. He could hear their voices a room away.

"When were you planning to tell me this need-to-know bit of information?" Jack Chaney's tone was brusque but not angry.

"I just found out myself. When they were doing the tests at the hospital." Tessa D'Angelo Chaney sounded defensive, then more emotional. "You're not happy, I take it."

"Happy? I come home from weeks in the field, filthy, tired and looking for nothing beyond a few days of mind-blowing sex and you drop the bomb that I'm going to be a daddy. Happy? Ecstatic is my new middle name."

There was a squeal of delight from her, followed by a long moment of silent communication. He took advantage of it to move stealthily into the hall. A sudden fearful cry from the direction of the girl's bedroom had him fading back into the shadows.

"I'll go," Chaney murmured.

"Don't be gone long. We have lots to discuss."

"On a more horizontal plane, I'm hoping."

"Chaney, you dog."

"No longer the lone wolf. I'm a pack animal now. And I'll be howling at the moon tonight."

Her chuckle was low and husky with expectation.

He heard Chaney move away. Then before he had a chance to take evasive action, Tessa came down the hall. He stood frozen, hoping she'd miss him in the darkness as she walked toward the kitchen. She was almost past him when she whirled, taking him completely by surprise with the pistol in her hand. He had no choice but to catch her wrist, spinning her back to front against him and clamping the other hand over her mouth to seal in any cry of warning. He wasn't fooled by her sudden capitulation, so he wasted no time with introductions. She was busy contemplating her next offensive move and the last thing he wanted was to hurt her.

"I'm not going to harm you or your family. I'm here to speak to your husband."

A low deadly drawl came from right behind him.

"Then you'd better talk fast and consider them your last words."

"I'm here on Barbara's behalf."

Apparently those were the magic words because

Tessa relaxed in his grasp and Chaney removed the unmistakable bore of a semiautomatic pistol from the base of his skull. The hall lights snapped on, blinding them all for an instant. Chaney stepped around into view to regard him narrowly.

"You must be McGee. I recognize you from photos." His hard dark glare fixed upon the placement of Tag's hands. "But if you don't let my wife go right now, that's all the pleasantries you're going to get from me."

Tag released her. She bolted away and Jack had her immediately stashed behind his back.

"To what do we owe this unexpected B and E?" Jack demanded in only a slightly more friendly tone.

"Sorry I couldn't wait for the formal invite. Chet Allen is out. He's behind the mysterious illness the children contracted in Chicago that by now, I'm sure, has been traced to some little-known drug out of Southeast Asia. He's been using threats against Tessa to intimidate Barbara. To get him to stop, I need to use some of your government connections."

"He's not going to scare me out of testifying." To prove her point, Tessa pushed free of her husband's sheltering arm to stand her ground. As she confronted him boldly, Tag was aware of one heart-stopping fact.

Barbara D'Angelo wasn't the only one her daughter resembled.

She looked like her father, too.

The ice-blue eyes glaring at him were his own.

Why hadn't Barbara told him?

Tessa frowned, perplexed by the intensity of his stare. Jack cut in to curtail her curiosity.

"What kind of help do you need? I'd kind of hoped we'd heard the last of Allen once we got him behind bars."

Tag tore his gaze away from Tessa's to concentrate on Jack's question. "Not yet. Maybe never if I can't figure out what he's up to."

"Where's Barbara?"

"With her parents in Florida. I called in a favor from a friend who owns a private plane. He flew me up on the QT. Barbara said you were a capable guy with a lot of connections."

Jack shrugged. "I know people who know people. I can make some calls if you tell me what you need to know."

"For starters, who sprang Chet from jail. Then I need behind-the-scenes intel on a Dr. Phillip Frye and retired Colonel Patrick Kelly. And whatever you can find out about the murder of a South Vietnamese colonel by the name of Tam Quan. And any details on the assassinations of Viet friendlies. I have a list." He provided the scribbled names that Claudia Calvin had taken down during his rambling recollections. Names that even now he couldn't associate with any faces or misdeeds. But he knew what they were. They were the names of the innocent people he'd killed.

"What are you looking for?"

"A link."

"To what? Or whom?"

"To me. And to whoever stood to profit from their deaths."

"I'll put on coffee," Tessa offered, more for practical purposes than to be a good hostess.

McGee watched her go, his thoughts in a tangle. His daughter. His and Barbara's. How had that happened? Well, he knew *how* it happened and probably when but not why she'd chosen to say nothing about it. She had to have known that he would have come running back to embrace the responsibility. She had to have known—

She had to have known, which was why she'd said nothing. Because it was never her intention for him to be the father of her child. That honor had gone to Robert D'Angelo, who had the potential to soar on the success meter.

Damn her.

Chaney sat him down in one of the posh interior rooms to wait while he made his overseas calls. Purposefully, Tag blanked his mind, forbidding himself to think or feel. His head pounded. Nausea built in his middle until his senses were swimming with it. He started to lower his head between his knees when he heard a low sniffling sound. He straightened, the movement waking huge swells of hot sickness. Through blurred vision, he saw a girl standing in the doorway. She clutched her pillow in front of her, her eyes still unfocused and dazed by the bad dream that had woken her and sent her looking for comfort from family. Vaguely, he registered the fact that this dark-hued South American child was somehow Tessa's daughter but his main focus was already rapidly slipping away, keyed by the plaintive sound of her weeping.

He heard sobbing, pleading, the words not in English but in Vietnamese.

The pain in his head was blinding. He squeezed his eyes shut and when he opened them, he saw great pools of blood surrounding the figure of a man. Over that prone and motionless body were two wailing children, their faces tear-streaked and twisted horribly by fear and grief as they begged for the return of their father. And for their lives. From him. The weight of his pistol hung heavy in his hand.

"Finish them." Chet Allen's command was cold and concise. "I'll see to the woman."

Helpless rage. Resistance. Spears of agony lancing through his head. He saw the pistol coming up in his hand as if held by another. Someone not controlled by his thoughts, his wants, his horror. The children sobbed all the louder, the noise echoing in his brain. *Don't look at them. Don't hear them. Follow the rules. The rules. Enemies must be neutralized.*

The boy, maybe all of six or seven, looked straight into his eyes, into his soul, as the pistol was leveled at his head. The recoil jerked in his hand. The sound of the shot recoiled in his mind.

"McGee? Can you hear me? Deep breath. Come on, man. Pull it together. I'm not in the mood to clean up puke on my floor at this time of night."

He dropped back into the yielding cushions of the couch as dry heaving spasms clenched through his belly. Dots of bright color swirled across the black veil of memory, intensifying, making him blink against the sear of truth.

What have I done? What kind of monster have I become?

Answers. Barbara needed answers. Who would know? Who was privy to what had happened to the three boys thrust into a violent manhood by a country at war? She racked her memory as she drove, not back toward Miami, but north into Virginia where Patrick Kelly ran an import business in Norfolk. She'd found his name doing research on the Internet at a small-town library after a fast-food breakfast. Then she'd rented a car to pursue what she needed to know.

What had happened a world away to so deeply scar those she'd loved and lost? If Kelly didn't have the solution, perhaps he held a clue.

She remembered him vaguely from the letters she'd gotten from Robert. He rarely mentioned the circumstances surrounding him in Southeast Asia. The focus of his communications was usually directed toward their future plans once he'd returned stateside. But she did recall his glowing remarks about the lieutenant who'd handpicked and groomed them for his unit. Kelly was on his second tour, a career man who considered it his duty to see that each and every man went home with him. Barbara remembered feeling safe after hearing that. Robert had relied on him, trusted him, admired him. That was good enough for her.

Kelly lived in an upscale home with enough acreage to estimate his worth at a number followed by an impressive parade of zeros. A group of sleek horses wheeled away from the fence at her approach and cantered across the enormous paddock.

She was met in the drive before the engine had even quieted by two serious-faced men in dark, nondescript clothing. They flanked the vehicle. She'd worked with Jack Chaney long enough to recognize hired security. The one on the left came to tap on her driver's door window. She rolled it down.

"Help you, ma'am?" he drawled.

"I'm here to see Patrick Kelly."

"Is the colonel expecting you?"

"That's all right, Paul," came a voice from the walkie-talkie clipped to his belt. "Have Mrs. D'Angelo come up."

The door was opened for her and Barbara was escorted by the two expressionless men to where their employer stood in the shadows of the front porch. Barbara understood. He was keeping himself from being a target. The armed men, the cautious attitude. Did he fear he was slated to follow Frye?

"Mrs. D'Angelo, I've been expecting you to come here looking for answers ever since I heard your name on the news."

She recognized him from some of the photos of their unit Robert had sent. The one she remembered was of the lieutenant in his makeshift quarters, grinning in front of a map of the area surrounding Hep Hung that was pinned by bayonets to his sandbag wall. She'd thought he looked so young to have such responsibility. Kelly waved her into his home with that same genuine smile.

"I'm sorry to disturb you, Colonel Kelly."

"Everything that's happened is disturbing," he countered with a shake of his head. "Robert's death. Now Frye's murder. I'm the one who's sorry you were drawn into this mess."

He led the way to a dark-paneled office made comfortable by its worn leather and horsey decor. She took the club chair he offered and let her anxieties ebb. Here was a man used to being in charge. And she was more than willing to be relieved of the burden.

"Is McGee with you?" At her immediate alarm, he calmed her with easy assurances. "We spoke two days ago, the morning of the murder. I filled him in on my part in an investigation of Frye's activities and he told me about Allen's agenda. I'm afraid that's about as far as we got. I've been following things on the news. Of course I don't believe for a second that McGee did the shooting. It was Allen, wasn't it?"

Her tired shoulders sagged with relief. "Yes, I think so. What I don't know is why."

"Allen is a very, very dangerous man. McGee and D'Angelo tried to help him over in 'Nam. Your husband got shot for his trouble."

"I don't understand."

"Allen found out about a drug-running network and he started doing for-hire assassinations for them. D'Angelo and McGee found out about it and tried to get him out of it. They went to Frye but unfortunately, the doctor was already up to his Hippocratic oath in that and other equally unsavory businesses. D'Angelo went to the authorities and was going to testify against

Allen. About that time, the three of them were out on patrol, and D'Angelo was mysteriously wounded and shipped home. No charges were ever brought against Frye or Allen, so whoever was controlling the strings must have had plenty of pull with the brass. I just wish they'd come to me. Why didn't they come to me?" He shoved his hand back through his cropped hair in a gesture of frustration. "I thought they trusted me. I could have helped them."

"Don't take it personally, Colonel. The three of them have always been an exclusive group. They would have tried to handle things between them without going to outsiders."

"I wasn't an outsider."

"I didn't think I was, either, but apparently that wasn't the case." She sighed heavily. "What are we going to do?

"Allen has to be neutralized."

Barbara winced at the casual way she referred to Chet's death, but she couldn't argue the necessity. Not with her family and Tag at risk.

"Can you get in touch with McGee?"

"I don't know where he is."

"Will he contact you?"

She considered the thirty years of silence, weighing it against the passion they'd shared just the night before. "I don't know. He took my cell phone. I tried calling earlier but he wouldn't pick up." And she hadn't left a message. Coward. The phone wasn't the only thing he'd taken from the hotel. He'd also stolen away her sense of balance.

"Try again. Have him meet you someplace isolated, someplace contained. Someplace where Allen will follow. Then, if McGee can't put him down, we can step in and finish it."

She nodded numbly. She was helping to arrange a murder. Even after Chet had killed Robert, had held her and her daughter at gunpoint, had threatened their safety and killed yet again, the thought of his cold-blooded execution made her queasy. The reality of Tag pulling the trigger to end the life of his friend made her nauseous. But Kelly was right. Chet had to be stopped.

"I know a place."

"Good."

"But what if they don't follow?"

"If you go, McGee will follow to make sure you're not in jeopardy. Allen won't want to miss the opportunity. You just have to make sure McGee understands the mission. Allen has to be put down. He can't be left alive. He can't be controlled. And as you've figured out for yourself by now, he's got enough pull to get himself out of any civilian court."

"You'll get Tag the help he needs?"

"Absolutely. My word on it. I don't like the idea of involving you."

"You didn't involve me. Chet did. Don't worry. Tag will make sure I'm safe. He'll be there to protect me." She had no doubts about that. Not a single one.

"Make the call."

Taking a deep breath, she took the receiver he passed to her. Her hand trembled as she dialed. Her own pert, professional voice answered. She made the message concise.

"Good." Kelly sat back in his chair with a grim smile. "I hate to see it come to this. Allen was a good man once. They all were good men."

"You didn't make the wrong choices for Chet. He did that himself."

"Still… If only there was a way to get through to him. But, I suppose it's too late for that. He's a time bomb who needs to be defused. He should have been after the conflicted ended. But he just wouldn't walk away like your husband and McGee did. He couldn't leave it behind."

"What?"

"The killing."

A soft sound from the doorway distracted them from their solemn conversation. A lovely Asian woman stood in the opening, her almond-shaped eyes glistening, her brightly painted lips working in distress.

"Su, I'm sorry you had to hear that." Kelly's voice was tender and filled with loving concern.

"I will be fine," she told him in a quavering voice. "Just as long as you keep your promise. As long as you find justice for my children. Tam was a casualty of war. I understand that. But the children… Why did they have to kill my children?" Her shoulders began to shake in the throes of remembered grief.

"They?" Barbara prompted.

"The two soldiers who came to our house. Allen and McGee."

Chapter 11

The buzz of the cell phone woke him. Sitting up, McGee felt a moment of disorientation. The walls of glass, the comfortable sofa, the scent of something drenched in mouthwatering Mexican seasonings. His stomach rumbled in response even as he struggled to acclimate himself.

Chaney's home. His and Barbara's daughter's.

His daughter's.

While that newly discovered emotion roiled through him, he rubbed his eyes so he could read his watch face. Six o'clock. He'd slept the afternoon away. Amazing considering how much preyed upon his mind. But realizing it had reached its limits, his body had just shut down, affording the much-needed time to recharge and refocus. Now, he was ready to take action. If only he knew what direction to take.

He caught a glimpse of movement. Tessa D'Angelo Chaney stood in the shadows of the room, watching him. Her expression was as stoic as his own.

"Are you him?"

Her question pierced his heart. "Depends on who *him* is."

She looked uncomfortably for a way to explain. "Did you and my mother have… Were the two of you…"

"Before I went into the service, your mother and I had a very special relationship." That was a bland way to paint the truth.

"Why didn't it last?" There was nothing subtle about that.

"We were also very young and didn't expect the complications that got in our way."

"Like what?"

"Life. Growing up. A war."

Her pale eyes, eyes so much like his own, began to shimmer in the faint light. "Why didn't you marry her?"

"I wanted to."

"Why didn't you want me?"

A bitter pill of anguish wedged in his throat, making her question stick and burn. "I didn't know about you until I first laid eyes on you today."

"And if you had?"

The arrival of the little girl, Rose, gave him a much-needed grace period before answering that question.

"It's dinnertime," the preteen announced. She

regarded Tag curiously but, with remarkable maturity, contained it.

Seemingly as eager to escape the conversation as he was, Tessa looped an arm about the girl's shoulders. "Whatever it is, it smells great. Constanza's cooking is the best thing about coming home." A sudden color warmed her cheeks as she admitted, "Well, almost." Then came her stiff offer. "Mr. McGee, you'll join us, of course."

"I have a call to take first. I'll be right there."

"Follow your nose."

When the two of them disappeared down one of the home's labyrinth of hallways, Tag released a ragged breath.

What would he have done had he known about Tessa? What could he have done if Barbara was determined to claim a society life that had been out of his reach? Fight the Calvins and all the power they wielded with their money and their connections?

The Calvins wouldn't have mattered, he realized then. He would have gone toe-to-toe with the devil himself had Barbara wanted to make it work between them. But she'd never given him that chance to prove himself. And now they would never know.

Wearily, he pulled the cell phone out of his jacket pocket. He didn't recognize the area code or number displayed on the LCD screen. But when he listened to the message, there was no mistaking the voice or the way his heart leaped in response to it.

"McGee, I'll meet you at the ranger station on Isle

Royale. It's time we brought our friend out into the open so we can end this."

His pulse raced.

What was she thinking, putting herself in Allen's path on the isolated island? Depending upon which one of them Chet was watching, she could wind up in those lonesome woods alone with a killer.

What was she thinking?

"I've got some news."

He looked up at Chaney's announcement, not quite quick enough to hide the desperation in his gaze.

"What?" Chaney asked.

"Barbara's gone to Isle Royale to force a confrontation with Allen. I've got to go. Now."

Chaney nodded and passed over the quickly scribbled notes he held in his hand. "Read these. See if they make any sense to you. It's about the investigation into Frye's bad habits and the money behind him. Makes for some interesting speculation. Then call me. I can be a handy fellow if you need someone at your back."

"Thanks."

"What's family for?"

Tag blinked. "How long have you known?"

"I dug up stuff about Tess's father that I wasn't too eager to share. Wasn't my place." Chaney fished an envelope out of his pocket. "Take this and read it when you're ready."

Tag glanced at the yellowed paper. It was addressed to him. In Barbara's handwriting. The postmark was more than three decades old.

"Where did you get this?"

"D'Angelo had it stashed with the evidence incriminating Allen and Martinez. I took the liberty of hanging on to it for safekeeping. Not a bad idea, since the rest of the materials mysteriously disappeared."

"Did you read it?"

Chaney shook his head. "Wasn't meant for me."

Tag took the letter. Tension chewed at the walls of his belly as he tucked it into his jacket. He wasn't sure he was up to any more surprises. At least, not yet.

"I've got to go."

"You'll be back." It was more of an order than a question.

"When this is over."

Chaney handed Tag the semiautomatic pistol he'd been ready to blow his head off with only hours ago. "Take this. Bring it back. It's one of my favorites."

McGee nodded, tucking the piece into his waistband at the small of his back. There was no more that needed to be said between two experienced warriors, so he walked out without another word. He'd be back, if for no other reason than to answer Tessa's question. She deserved that answer from him.

The brisk hike back to where he'd parked the SUV, rented under his alias, Arthur McAffee, gave him a chance to do some clear thinking.

His daughter. He knew nothing about her, other than that they shared the same eye color and that she was as tough as her mother was tender. How much more he learned was up to the two of them. It didn't matter that Barbara hadn't wanted to introduce them. It didn't, but then again, it did.

His daughter. His and Barbara's. A strange shaky joy took hold of him and wouldn't let go. Like discovering what you wanted most under the Christmas tree.

Why hadn't Barbara told him? Why had she denied him the chance to watch his only child grow up, even from an impersonal distance? If he'd had something like that to cling to over these past years, perhaps he wouldn't have spent them in a foggy limbo punctuated only by unrealized hopes and terrifying dreams.

His daughter.

But then again, maybe it wasn't such a good idea for her to get to know him. At least, not until this business with Chet was finished. Then maybe he could recover some sort of life worth living.

He drove hard. He crossed the bridge in the darkness and was welcomed back to the wooded frontier of Michigan's Upper Peninsula. He had coffee in St. Ignace while he gassed up the vehicle and then pushed on through the sporadic towns set amid dense forests and stone, wondering with every mile if he was ahead of or behind Barbara. And Chet. Wondering if he'd have the chance to set the scene for this, their final confrontation.

Five and a half hours later, he had breakfast in Copper Harbor. He finally read through the papers Chaney had given him and made a quick call to his son-in-law. His son-in-law. That idea kind of sneaked up on him, too. And he found he liked it. Then he sat back to finish his eggs, letting things fall into place as he waited for dawn to make the trip over Lake Superior to the island where he'd hidden away from the world. Now, that ugly, violent world was coming to his door and he had no option but to face it.

And to face Barbara with the truth she'd hidden from him for far too long.

Her letter remained unopened in his pocket. He had no problem racing to his possible death, but he hadn't the courage to receive her words. Not yet.

She was there in the ranger station where he'd lived alone for the past seven years. She sat in the front office, not in his private quarters, and from the deep circles beneath her eyes when she looked at him questioningly, he could tell she'd had as little sleep as he had.

"Ranger Todd let me stay the night. I told him you knew I was coming. I hope that was all right."

Her voice was low and gritty with fatigue. And as invitingly sexy as the unkempt tousle of her hair. He fought against the urge to cross the room to pull her into his arms, to absorb the oh-so-right feel of her next to the hurried beat of his heart. That distance was too great to span.

"I got your message."

She nodded. Her shoulders rose and fell with the magnitude of her distress and the fear she was trying to hide. Shaky fingers tunneled back through her hair. "Is he out there someplace?"

"Not yet. At least not according to Sam at the docks. No one's rented a boat or come over on the ferry. Except you."

"But he will."

"Yes."

Again, the jerky nod. Her gaze touched on him with a furtive, almost apprehensive flicker. And suddenly, he realized that part of her fear was of him.

"Where did you go when you left me?"

The polite question didn't address what was really bothering her, but it was a start.

"To make sure your family was all right."

Her posture snapped erect. Her huge eyes demanded to know.

"They're fine. Chaney's with them."

Just as she started to relax, he delivered his next quietly presented question.

"Why didn't you tell me?"

She didn't look surprised or alarmed. She seemed relieved. Her soft gray eyes glazed over with unshed tears. It took her a moment to speak, and when she was finally able to, her voice was thready with emotion.

"I did. I sent you a letter. And I waited and waited to hear from you, for you to come home. But I didn't. And you didn't." There was no accusation, only a sad resignation underlined by the quicksilver trace of moisture trickling down her cheeks. He could see in the brief contortion of her features the devastating heartbreak of the girl he'd left behind to face an uncertain future alone. She thought he hadn't cared. And all his anger fell away.

"This letter?" He produced it and gave her a second to recognize it before adding, "Chaney found it in Rob's things. I never got to read it, Barb. I never had any idea until I saw Tessa."

She gulped down a sob and closed her eyes, sending a flood of dampness coursing down her face. "I never heard from you. I thought…I believed what he told me."

"What who told you?"

"Robert." She forced his name past the clog of anguish in her throat. "He told me you didn't want the responsibility."

He couldn't keep the hurt from his tone when demanding, "How could you think that? Even for a minute?"

She shook her head, looking up at him through eyes dazed by guilt and grief. "I was seventeen. I was still in high school. I never got your letters. My father intercepted them. Burned them. When Robert came home on leave and told me that—that my news had scared you away, what else could I believe? I hadn't heard from you at all. I was three months pregnant. I didn't know what else to do. Then Robert offered to marry me instead, to give my baby a name."

"So you wouldn't disappoint your family."

She winced at that harsh summary but didn't deny it. "The scandal would have destroyed them."

"Better I take the fall, right? Disappointment was nothing new to me."

She stared him straight in the eye with a directness that unnerved him as she spoke. "They wouldn't have let me keep the baby. Your baby. And I couldn't stand losing that part of you. I would have done anything. I let Robert go to my parents and tell them the baby was his. They were angry but he told them a quick marriage to a man about to go overseas in the service of his country wouldn't be too terrible a mark on their careers."

"Not the way marriage to me would have been."

"No," she all but whispered. "Robert promised to provide for me and the baby, to give us both a secure and respectable future, as long as I never told my child. As long as I never let anyone know that we weren't a happy family. I kept my promise and he kept his. I was seventeen. I believed him."

"You believed his lies," Tag corrected, the razor edge of his frustration and fury slicing across his words. She bowed her head in repentant misery, so he added more softly, "We both did. And we let him steal whatever happiness we might have had together."

She looked up then, blinking away the tears, saying, "Not yet. Not now that we know the truth."

"It's too late."

His pronouncement was crushing. She didn't know how to resist its weight. Her body sagged beneath it as Tag continued.

"We can't go back, Barb, not with all this baggage between us. We come from different worlds. All those things that stood between us as kids still stand between us now. You've lived the life you wanted with no regrets. I don't even have a past to remember. I don't know what kind of man I became while I was over there. Maybe just what your father predicted. A man just like Chet. I won't let you ruin your future with a man like that."

Before she could argue, before he could weaken to anything she might say, he walked away from the pleading look in her eyes, from the offer of a life he'd always dreamed of, with her.

He stalked the woods, not straying too far from the station but not ready to go back inside. News of Robert's treachery cut him like the slash of an enemy's bayonet to the gut. How could he have done such a thing, knowing what Barbara meant to him? Knowing the plans and hopes they'd held? But then Rob had made no secret of how he felt about Barbara, that if he thought he'd had a chance, he would have tried to win her away. But he hadn't been able to compete with the passion, with the soul-deep connection his best friend found with the girl of all their dreams. Even though Rob was her parents' pick, she'd chosen Taggert McGee with his quiet strength and troubled past. And Tag thought Rob had gotten over it.

Apparently not.

They were from the same mold, sharing the same ambitions. That's what Rob had told him when he returned with a wedding ring on his finger. Once there was some breathing distance between them, Barbara had realized that what she felt for Tag was just raging hormones that had calmed down over the two-month separation. That's what Rob had told him.

He'd said Barbara welcomed his attention and was willing to build upon the bond they'd begun when they'd first dated. Before she and Tag struck like flint on steel. Before she'd gotten sidetracked by lust and left common sense behind.

Robert had seen her first, dated her first and despite the fling she'd had with his best friend, he'd married her in a quick civil ceremony before rejoining his unit to be shipped out overseas.

That's what Rob had told him and he'd believed every damn word without question. Because he'd been young, too. And because he knew Rob was the better bargain where Barbara Calvin was concerned.

He slumped back against the trunk of a fragrant pine and drew the crumpled letter out once more. It was addressed to him but the hands that had opened it weren't his own. Robert had read the words meant for him and had stepped in to claim the future he was supposed to have had. Wasn't it about time he found out what Barbara had had to say?

The envelope contained two handwritten pages that would have changed his life if he'd read them three decades earlier.

"My love," it began. The ghost of a bittersweet smile touched his lips. "I miss you so much. I think of you every minute of every day and the thought of you going into danger makes me cry myself to sleep each night. I guess I won't get much rest until you return to share my bed and our dreams."

He let the pages drop for a moment, having to blink hard to focus enough to see her neatly penned sentiments.

"I have some news," the letter continued. Her penmanship was not quite as perfect. "I hope you'll think it's as fabulous as I do. I know we had talked about starting a family much later. Unfortunately, little Kyle or Tessa (names I've picked, but we can talk about that) isn't going to wait."

He read on, his heart swelling, his eyes filling with every optimistic word. Their baby. And she couldn't wait to share every detail with him so he wouldn't feel he'd missed out on the magical experience.

"Please don't be too upset. I know the timing could be better, but now I'll have a piece of you to hold on to and I won't be so alone. I love you enough to wait forever but I can't wait to see you when you come home on leave. We'll have to tell my parents and your family, which won't be pretty, but we can face it together and it won't be so bad. We'd talked about marriage when you got out, but under the circumstances I'm ready to say I do the minute you get here. I can't wait to start our life together. We'll make it work. I love you. I love you. I love you."

He squeezed his eyes shut, hearing her sweet voice stating that over and over in his head. Seeing the tears on her brave face at the bus station. It shouldn't have been so easy to cast that claim aside to believe the worst his betraying friend had to say.

And Barbara, waiting to hear from him, waiting to learn how he received the news. Then, thinking his love was so shallow he could desert her and their child. How hurt and frightened she must have been, facing that emptiness and pain with just good old Rob and his offer of security to bail her out.

And how hurt she would be now if he walked away from what he was feeling for her and their daughter now that he knew the truth.

That wasn't the kind of man he was. And he would tell her so.

Folding the letter with care, he returned it to his pocket. Time to face that part of the past he remembered.

And that's when the cold muzzle of a Glock touched his temple.

"Hey, buddy. Time we had us a little talk."

Chapter 12

Careful not to react with any surprise, Tag murmured, "I've been expecting you."

Slowly he turned so that the bore of the pistol centered right between his eyes. He stared past it into the gloating stare of Chet Allen.

"Want to tell me what this is all about, Chet? I've never been as good at games as you and Rob."

"And Barbie. Don't forget sweet little Barbara. She's the one who played us all from the beginning."

Tag took a risk and spoke with a curt annoyance. "No she didn't, Chet. There was never any question about who she preferred."

Chet's gaze narrowed, then he smiled good-naturedly. "You won, hands down. At least until Robby decided to cheat to steal the prize."

"You knew? You knew what he did?" Just when he thought the sense of betrayal couldn't go any deeper.

"How do you think I got Robby to drop his holy war investigation over there in 'Nam? I couldn't have him pulling the plug when I was having so much fun. Told him if he ever said a word, I'd tell you the little bun Barbie had in the oven was all yours. He knew what you would have done. Probably deserted just to get back to her. I tried the same threat a few months ago, but he wasn't buying into it then. He figured it was water under the bridge after thirty or so years. But he was wrong, wasn't he? She's still the only one, isn't she? I was counting on that. My contacts are good, but I just couldn't flush you out. Until I mentioned Barb and you came popping out of that hole you'd been hiding in, just like I knew you would."

He shook his head and gave a mystified little laugh. "Same old Mac. Remember the three of us? The planner, the doer and the dreamer. Nothing's changed. Except we have to make our own plans now."

"What do you want, Chet? If you wanted to take me out, you could have done that any number of times. I haven't been exactly low-profile. Why play all the games? Just finish the job you were hired to do. Or is that job over now that Frye is dead? Were those your fingerprints on that?"

"I wouldn't have wasted a bullet on that mind-twisting pig. But I didn't stop it, either." He lowered the gun. "The game hasn't been the same without you to play it with me, Mac."

"Sorry, but I'm going to sit this one out, too."

Chet chuckled. "I don't think so. Not after Kelly went to so much trouble to get the three of us here. You kill me, I kill you, doesn't matter. It's a win-win situation for him."

"Kelly? What's he got to do with this?"

"Only…everything. Did you really think Frye was smart enough to pull off such a sweet deal in 'Nam? He was just a tool. Kelly was the man. He set up the targets and had Frye point us in the right direction. He had to work on you, you with your honor and nobility. Hell, I would have done it if they'd just asked."

His laugh was chilling. Looking at him, McGee could no longer envision the pal he'd sneaked into horror movies with, the companion who'd shared his tent at night where they read comic books and pretended they weren't hiding out from having to go home, where the violence was horrible. The fearless friend who'd enlisted in a war he cared nothing about because he couldn't stand to see his only two buddies leave without him. Where had that man gone? What stood here in his place was a…monster.

"Yes, sir, we did the dirty work so Kelly got what he wanted—more than his cut of the drug trade—and Frye made sure he never told anyone what he'd discovered about the black market flesh trafficking he was doing."

"What did Kelly want?"

"What does any man want? Power, money and a babe. Only his babe belonged to someone else, to someone who thought he was his friend. See an uncomfortable parallel there?"

Tag gaped at him. "Kelly had us kill Tam Quan so he could have his wife? Is that what this is all about?"

"She saw us on the news and she demanded Kelly do something about us. Of course, she didn't know her new hubby was behind her becoming a widow. So Kelly arranged for me to get out on bail so he could erase the little problem of your questionable memory. He knew I wasn't going to say anything. No percentage in it for me. But you, he wasn't so sure about."

Chet scowled, displaying a rare bit of true emotion. "Why didn't you just see Frye before you checked out of 'Nam? He would have wiped your slate clean and you would have been out of it for good. Now, you've put me in a position I really didn't want to be in. Dammit, Mac. I don't want to kill you."

"But you will."

Chet paused, then shrugged, his nonchalance back in place. "You know I will. Nothing personal when the job's involved."

"And Barbara and Tessa, you're going to kill them, too?"

"That's up to me. I like that girl. She's got your grit and integrity. If Robby had spawned her, I wouldn't have hesitated."

"If you're looking for a way out, let me help you find it."

Allen gave him a crooked smile. "Too late for that, buddy. I'm damaged goods. No amount of psych time in the VA is going to change anything for me. I like what I do. It's the only thing I've ever been better at than the two of you."

"This isn't a competition, Chet."

"Isn't it? Think again. Only I was never supposed to win the game. You should have seen how surprised Robby was. Priceless. He deserved what he got, the sanctimonious bastard. He only had a conscience when it was convenient. Not like you. Yours beat you up daily, and I hated to see you suffer for it. But what could I do? Who the hell would believe anything I had to say?"

"I would. And I bet we could convince a lot of influential people."

"Why would I want to do that, Mac? Just so they can throw me in some funny farm and let me turn into a turnip? I'd rather go out in style."

"And you want me to do that little favor for you. Is that why you brought Barb into this?"

Chet grinned. "I didn't think you'd oblige me if I just asked. And then again, what fun would that be? You and me, we've always been simpatico. We're evenly matched in skills, if not in morals. What do you say? Wanna play the most dangerous game with me?"

The man was clearly insane.

"No. I'm not going to play."

"Even to save pretty little Barbie's life? Oh, I bet you will. See, the thing is, the only way I'm going to get out of this is if one of us is dead. If I take you out, their rogue is gone and they'll tuck me undercover and let me work for a long, long time in some foreign dung heap. My threats against Kelly will make that happen. But if you take me down, then you go public with what you now know is the truth. You're the hero, get the girl, and Kelly gets his just deserts. I'm okay with that, too. You play the game and you play it hard, Babs and her family are safe. What do you say?"

"I say we stick together and blow this thing wide open, the two of us. That's the last thing any of them would expect."

Chet smiled, the gesture sad and jaded. "That's not going to happen. I'd still go to jail. I can't do that, Mac. Not even for you."

"You think they'll believe me? They've got me classified me as a Grade A nutball with a gun."

"Barbie's folks will make believers of them. And she and that tough little daughter and her hard-ass husband will stand right beside you at your press conference. Plus, I have this." He held up a key. "Robby wasn't the only one who kept a locker at the gym in Roseville. Remember how little Barbie used to go there in her daddy's convertible to watch us spar? She'd sit there in that tease of a miniskirt getting off on the sweat and the blood. I've always had a fondness for that place and those times. They were good times, weren't they, Mac?" He looked far away for a moment, then focused back on the key. "There are some interesting things in there. Tapes Frye kept of our sessions when he'd clean our memories of the things we'd done so we could live with ourselves afterwards. Robby was the only one of us who never remembered anything. Lucky him."

"Chet, you don't have to do this."

"But I want to."

That summed it up for Chet Allen.

"Then just shoot me now and go back to Kelly a hero." He braced himself mentally and physically as Allen weighed the gun at his side.

"That wouldn't be fair, now would it? And you're the only one who's always played fair with me, Mac. Always. We'll start our game at dawn. I like the symbolism of that. Then I'll come after you to finish things, ready or not. I'll be watching. Don't think of calling for help, either. I took out your radio antenna and we both know there are no cell towers for a relay. It's just the three of us now. And if I were you, I'd be using those hours between now and then to be making up for lost time with Barbie girl. Ticktock, Mac. Get busy."

So this was his world?

Barbara moved about the station and the sparse rooms in the back, trying to get a feel for the man Taggert McGee had become. It was all about business. Maps, memos, some gorgeous wilderness photography, but nothing personal. No pictures or mementos. No television or newspaper to connect him to the outside. He probably wouldn't have heard about Robert's death while existing in this self-imposed isolation. The loneliness of it made her melancholy. The only thing linking him back to the boy she'd loved was the books. Stacks and stacks of literature and poetry. Deeply intellectual reads that he'd loved to sink his wisdom teeth into. He might have become a college professor had his number not come up in the draft. He might have become her husband and the father of her child. And they might have been so happy.

He'd never known about her situation, about Tessa. The shock of that turned her entire life upside down with a plague of what-ifs. What if she'd trusted him more and Robert less? What if she'd gone that extra mile to contact him, to see for herself that he didn't want the future her pregnancy created? But she'd had no reason not to trust those around her, no resources to check what they said against what she felt in her heart. Not then. Not after the pain of abandonment had eased to an almost tolerable ache. She had loved him so much; knowing his child was inside her had been the only thing that had kept her going. Could they have made it, the three of them, if she'd stood firm upon her promises those thirty years ago?

Could they make it now with the scars of misunderstanding disfiguring the truth for so long?

Tag didn't think so. He had no reason to have faith in what she felt for him, in what they'd felt for one another. But if that was true, if he didn't care enough to risk his heart, why was he here, risking his life? Not to save his own. He was too good at what he did. He could have faded from sight for another thirty years without anyone ever finding him. He'd only become visible because of her.

She paced back into the front of the station to wait for his return. As the hour grew later, her anxiousness increased with the surrounding darkness.

Where was he? Why did he stay away for so long? Was it his intention to deny her the chance to explain herself, to explore the ramifications of the truth now told? Or didn't it matter?

What if Chet Allen had already found him? What if she'd led him directly to his death? Was Allen out there even now, plotting, taking pleasure in planning her demise? Hers and Tessa's. Tension gripped her, twisting, knotting her insides until she was a coil of apprehension. When a scuffle of noise on the front porch sounded, it was enough to send her into a panic.

Who was out there? Friend or deadly foe?

She waited, breath panting from her. More scratching. The scraping of chairs on the wood flooring. The crash of a clay pot. She caught back a scream. Then reason took over. She wouldn't have heard Tag or Chet coming for her. They were professionals, used to silent stalking. This was…what exactly?

Cautiously, she moved to the door, snapping on the porch light. The sound stopped then was followed by a snuffling cry of distress. Peering out from a modest crack, she saw the cause of her concern. A black bear cub, no bigger than a pup, was rooting through the spilled dirt from the planter, looking for food.

"You're just a baby," Barbara cooed, then glanced around the shadowed perimeter. "Where's your mama?"

The cub stopped to regard her through bright button eyes, then gave a pitiful bawl of hunger. The universal tone of a young one in discomfort melted her heart.

"Are you out here all alone?" Still no sign of Mama Bear. Knowing she should wait for Tag's return, she started to close the door when the cub came ambling toward her without fear. It clawed at the door, making more of the pathetic wails for attention. It was hungry, alone and looking for care anywhere it could find it.

It had come to the right place.

Tag found the two of them in front of the fireplace. Barbara was feeding the cub oatmeal and honey from her fingers. The sight of her sitting cross-legged on the floor, swaddled in one of his wool flannel shirts, nursing a greedy baby, caused the last of his reserve to collapse. An image of Barbara caring for the child they had created burned in his hopes and dreams. And the pain of missing that sight and others like it welled up inside, filling all the empty niches in his aching soul with longing. He should have been there. For her. For Tessa. But there was no going back to claim those memories enjoyed by another.

"That's probably not a good idea."

She looked up, startled, then offered a small, slightly defiant smile. "He was hungry."

"He is a wild animal, not a pet."

"He's a baby who got separated from his mother."

Tag closed the door behind him and sighed morosely. "His mother is dead. A poacher got her. I found the other cub last week. It got attacked by some other predator. I didn't know what had happened to this little guy."

Her gaze glimmered with upset. She stroked the bristly coat as the cub, its belly full and rounded, curled up at her feet to fall fast asleep. "Will he make it without her?"

Tag shrugged. "Maybe. He seems to take to you. That's a good sign. I've got some contacts with animal rescue groups. They might be able to take him in. He's too little to be out there alone."

"No one should have to be that alone." She said it softly, with shades of meaning deep enough for him to drown in.

As she tucked her expensive cashmere sweater about the slumbering creature and placed him in the safe surround of the empty fire box, he got a glimpse of what he might have had and held dear. Not Barbara Calvin, the sweetly naive teen, but this woman, bereft of makeup and designer clothing, clad in his flannel shirt, fitting into the life he'd made for himself with an un-complaining aplomb. She'd always had a tender spot for strays, so patient, so overflowing with compassion for the most unfortunate. She'd looked right past his family flaws, ignoring his deficits to find and encour-age the strengths of the boy he'd been. Perhaps she could work that same magic on the lonely man he'd become. This was the tender woman who'd won his heart.

She looked up then, her soft gaze warm with care and optimism, and his words just burst out from his unguarded heart.

"I never stopped thinking about you, dreaming about you. Loving you."

For a moment, she didn't react and he experienced a terrible anguished panic. He was too late.

Then, she rose up from her cross-legged position on his floor and came to him without a word. He stood there, frozen in place, afraid to hope, afraid to breathe. Her palms skimmed up either side of his immobile face, cradling him in that gentle vee while she spoke the answer that fed his soul.

"Neither did I."

Their kisses started slow, with a poignant reacquainting heat that quickly took flame, engulfing them and forging them into one. One heart, one need, one goal. To span those missing years, to fill those lonely spots left achingly empty while they had been apart.

The feel of him, so hard, so lean, so…hers, fed the fantasies Barbara had harbored. Her mouth opened to their deepening passions, her heart opened to long dormant joy. She learned the angles of his face made harsh by the years, first with her fingertips and then with the sweep of her lips. And because she wasn't that young, inexperienced girl who'd last known him, she savored each sensation to the fullest. The rough burr of his cheek, the soft swell of his lower lip, the encouraging caress of his hurried breaths upon her neck until she swallowed them again with a needy urgency. The taste of him, remembered and renewed, hot, spicy, intoxicatingly delicious. Finally, out of breath, she simply leaned into him, upon those long, tough planes that had always surrendered such a sense of security.

"We've got until daybreak before we have to deal with Chet," he whispered, the enticement of that claim stirring her heart and her hopes.

"We've wasted enough time, don't you think, to let even a minute get away."

Because they both knew these hours until dawn might be their last.

He took her by the hand, leading her from the office area into his private quarters. With the lights off, with the overwhelming heat of him beside her, she didn't notice the starkness that had so disturbed her before. He tugged the covers off his bed and then they undressed each other, their actions becoming more and more frantic with the shedding of each layer until they were skin to skin, soul to soul.

And it was wonderful.

He took her down to the mattress, to the cozy flannel of his bottom sheet, leveling over her to form a warm, enveloping cover. This was what she'd yearned for in her marriage bed, this intensity of feeling that just kept getting bigger until she was filled to bursting. Her nerve endings were alive and tingling. Her blood sang through her veins with each anticipating beat of her heart. She couldn't keep her hands still, desperate to chart the rugged contours of his shoulders, his arms, his back, his flanks beneath her restless palms. He felt so good. He returned touch for touch, joy for joy, until she panted for fulfillment.

Then, with him filling her body, her spirit, her heart so completely, they moved together, creating a sweet, hot friction.

Building, sharpening, to a sudden explosive reward that left them both breathless and unable to guard against the wealth of emotions freed upon that spectacular release.

They lay quietly curled together in the darkness, sharing their heat, their sated happiness, and would have done so contentedly for the remainder of the night if they had had that luxury.

"Chet gave me until morning."

Barbara sat up with a gasp. "What? You spoke to him? He's here? Why didn't you tell me?"

Because selfishly, greedily, he'd wanted this moment alone with her. But he couldn't tell her that. Instead, he said, "While I keep him busy, I want you to head for the boat landing. I want you to hide there, stay out of sight until the first ferry comes across. Then I want you to go straight to the first phone and call Jack."

She just stared at him, her gaze incomprehensive. "You want me to leave you here alone with Chet?"

"Yes."

"He could kill you."

It didn't matter, as long as she was safe. But he didn't tell her that, either.

"Promise you'll go and won't look back."

He'd asked her to do pretty much the same thing thirty years ago. To let him go and go about her own life. Only, what kind of life would she have without him in it? She'd already lived a shallow existence, living her lonely days and nights for others. With nothing for herself. She couldn't…wouldn't go back to that.

"No."

"What?"

"No. We're in this together, McGee. I'm not going to let you walk away from me again."

"Barb, you don't—"

"I understand just fine. If Chet is waiting for some shoot-'em-up at dawn, then we'll have to slip away when he doesn't expect it. I was wrong to listen to Colonel Kelly. Chet is their problem, not yours."

"Kelly? When did you talk to Kelly?" Tag sat up, clutching her soft shoulders. She couldn't see the seriousness of his expression but felt the intensity in his firm grip.

"He encouraged me to come here. So you and Chet could face off. So you could—"

"Cover up his involvement."

She went very still. "You remember?"

She sounded so aghast that he was instantly suspicious. "What do I know, Barb? What did he tell you?"

When she didn't answer, he touched her face with questing fingertips. Her features worked with anguish. He felt the dampness of her tears.

"Barbara, what aren't you telling me?"

"I met his wife, his Vietnamese wife. She knew you and Chet. She recognized you both as the soldiers who…"

"Who what?" he prompted fiercely.

"As the men who killed her family."

The sound of a shot thundered through his head. He squeezed his eyes shut to contain the harsh reverberations.

Finish them.

He could hear Chet's cold command, could see the youthful face lifted up to him in fearful supplication. The horror of it chilled his soul. But what was worse was telling the woman he loved what he'd become.

"I killed them, Barb. I think I killed them."

Chapter 13

She didn't recoil from his torturous confession. She should have. She should have pulled away with the same disgust and outrage he felt inside. But instead, she fit one tender palm to his cheek.

"It wasn't you."

How could she say such a thing?

"Barbara, I've killed people. Innocent people."

"No, you haven't."

"Aren't you listening to me?" He was wildly angry, at her for the compassion shimmering in her stare, at himself for wanting to get lost in her absolving care. Both were wrong. And he'd been caught up in too many wrong things to let this one go. "I killed that woman's husband and her kids. I did."

A terrible truth wrenched from the heart of her as she cried, "I don't care. I don't care what you may have done. You can't change what's happened. I'm not going to lose you again. I won't." Her voice broke. She swallowed her fear and panic before continuing in a more reasonable tone. "Facing Chet won't bring those people back."

"But it will return my honor."

She laughed harshly at his somber declaration. "What's honor compared to your life?"

"Everything."

"Not to me."

He touched her damp cheek, soothing away the tears the way he'd like to ease her anguish.

"Barb, I have to do the right thing. You don't understand what it's like to live all those years with the fear that what's just beyond what you recall is a horror too big to be imagined. Like an empty shell, with no heart, no soul, only the ghost of your past."

She covered his hand with hers. "Yes, I do. I've waited thirty years to have you back, thirty years to come alive again, to feel, to love, to know happiness. I am not going to throw that away because you feel responsible for what was done to you without your knowledge and against your will."

He sighed wretchedly. "I'm not the hero you want me to be."

"Yes, you are."

And there, shining in her eyes, was the uncompromising belief he'd craved for so long. That simple claim eased a spirit tormented by doubts, by fears, by half-remembered demons. He let her continue without protest or objection, needing the healing balm of her support.

"We've already lost so much time, time we could have shared watching our daughter grow into a truly wonderful woman. You'll like her, Tag. She's so much like you."

He tucked his head so she wouldn't see the pain of that loss in his eyes, the desperate wanting to have that stolen time back. She went on in a soft, regretful voice that amazingly held none of the bitterness burning like acid in the back of his throat, in his belly, in his heart.

"I've spent those years living up to a bargain made under false pretenses, because of a lie, because of Robert's competitive greed to have anything he coveted. I was a symbol, not a person, to him. I was a means to what he wanted for himself and he was willing to compromise friendship and loyalty and truth to have me. And I don't think he ever forgave himself for it. I thought it was me, that it was his shame over what I'd done with you that made him so distant toward me and Tessa. But it was his own guilt. It was the lie he'd made us live.

"He was a good provider, Tag. He gave us everything we could want or need. Everything but love. He never knew how to do that where Tessa and I were concerned. Our boys, yes, but he couldn't breach that gulf with us. Tessa blamed me for it, and I'd promised Robert I would never tell her the truth. So, you see, our pasts aren't so very different. What you don't remember and what I couldn't have made us two lonely people living half a life. Because we weren't strong enough then to believe in the goodness, the rightness, of what we had, we couldn't take a risk."

"What risk?" he whispered.

"The risk it would take to fulfill that promise we made to each another the night before you left. It frightened me then. But it doesn't now. I don't care where you came from. I don't care what you did. I only know who you are. You are the father of my child. You are the man who's held my heart forever. And I want you. I want you to make good on that promise."

Then came his tortured reply. "I don't know if I can."

"You mean, if you want to." Pain saturated those words, hanging heavy on his conscience.

"No," he corrected quietly. His hand framed her lovely face. His thumb rode its delicate angles, now taut with misery. "I don't know if Chet will let me. I can't let him hurt you or your family."

"Your family, Tag. Your family, too."

He swallowed that truth, suffering for the way it seemed to wedge in sideways to dam all his emotions behind it.

"Barb—"

"Don't give him that kind of power over us. You don't have to play his game any more. Tessa and Rose are safe. I'm here with you. He's on an island, your island. He can't escape. Let the law or his own people have him. We can go somewhere, start over."

"Barb—"

She shook her head, not wanting to hear the somber facts he was about to speak. She was crying without being aware of it.

"Barb," he repeated gently. "We can't walk away from this. I'm wanted for murdering Frye. We can't just start over. I won't live another lie with you. It wouldn't be fair to either of us. If we start over together, it's got to be with a clean slate. You know that. You couldn't go on the run with me, leaving your daughter, your sons, your grandchildren behind. It's no kind of life for you."

"No kind of life is posing for cameras, smiling at guests you don't even know, watching every word you say because it will be in the papers the next day. It's tailored clothes and uncomfortable shoes, and a day planner that's on overdrive so you have no time to think or relax or enjoy what you have. But what you have gives you no joy. I want that joy, McGee. I haven't had it since you went away. Don't take it from me again."

He kissed her softly, slowly, with infinite care. She tasted of tears and poignant longing. And love.

And that's what he'd been missing.

He leaned back to murmur, "We have to get this behind us before we go on. You know that, don't you?"

She gave a jerky nod.

"I can't share my life with you until it's my own."

Again the reluctant nod, followed by the quiet hitch of a sob.

He drew her up to him, lying back so she was pillowed on his shoulder, cradled in the circle of his arms. He could feel the shivers of her weeping but was powerless to give them ease. So he simply held her, absorbing the glorious sensation of her against him while his mind spun agilely ahead in search of a solution.

After a time, her crying ended. She stayed within the curl of his embrace, but there was no relaxation in the luxurious line of her. His woman. The mother of his child.

He took a breath, expelling his tension with it. He let his mind quiet, his soul calm, his body still. There was a way. There had to be. She was counting on him to find it. He visualized their situation, plotting out the obstacles, the strengths and weaknesses, the way he had when far afield in the war. When careful planning meant the difference between survival and a nasty death. He knew the island. He knew the stakes, those cruelly high stakes. He knew Chet Allen. They'd hunted and tracked together as boys. They'd mapped out defensive plays in high school. They'd made it through the jungles on sheer nerve and wit. This was what they were both good at. All they were good at. The game. The rules differed. The reward changed. But it was still the game of outsmarting, outplanning and overpowering a targeted enemy. Then it occurred to him.

"Barb, are you up for a hike?"

She lifted her head to search out his features in the darkened room. "Now?"

"Soon. While it's still dark. We'd have to move fast and silent over some ugly ground. You'd have to keep up a brutal pace."

She was alert and anticipating. "I can keep up." The warmth of her chuckle caressed his bare chest. "All those politically correct aerobics classes." She was still for a moment, then asked, "What are you thinking?"

"I'm thinking that if we get far enough ahead of him and if he follows, which he will, maybe, just maybe we can end this without bloodshed." His voice lowered to a gravelly cadence. "I don't want to have to kill him, Barb. He's been my friend for as long as I can remember."

She rubbed a hand over his hard abdomen, feeling a slight quiver beneath her palm.

"We should get some sleep while we can."

Her hand drifted lower in response to his suggestion. His voice grew slightly strained.

"Or not."

His eyes closed, but not to seek rest or anything like it. Her touch wasn't that of a shy young woman on her first exploration. She knew exactly what she was doing and what it was doing to him. He lay quietly except for the urgent increase in his breathing. He stayed still except for the sudden laboring of his next breaths. He let her coax shivery spikes of sensation beneath her clever fingers, with the slow teasing curl of her tongue, with the wild, swirling suction of her mouth, until he couldn't stand the pleasure of it.

He pulled her up to where he was hungry for the taste of her lips, devouring them like a starving man. She slid over him, letting her hot, welcoming center take him in and hold him tight. Like coming home. He savored the reunion for a long, grateful moment. And then she began to move. Riding him at a slow, gliding pace, covering that uneasy ground between them with determined strides, bringing them closer, closer, closer to what they'd always wanted, needed from one another. Not the sex, though that was spectacular. Not the surprising explosion of fulfillment that brought previous expectations to their knees. But the calm after the storm. The soul-deep satisfaction of being together as completely and intimately as a man could be with a woman. A joining of hearts and spirits into one beautiful whole. A private place they'd found with one another, a paradise exclusive to only them. Their personal Eden. Their Shangri-la.

Entwined in body and mind, they slept briefly and woke to a new determination. Because there was something to live for, well worth the fight to hold on to. Because life was suddenly all the more precious for both of them.

They washed up together in Tag's tiny shower, the exercise one of binding intimacy rather than a sensual overture. They dressed quickly, in the darkness, Tag in commando attire and Barbara in a moisture-wicking jog suit. As they consumed microwave coffee and power bars, Tag laid out the plan.

When he was sure all her questions were answered, he readied for war, strapping on a wicked hunting knife and feeding cartridges into his rifle and into a pair of pistols. He tucked one pistol into his waistband and handed the other to Barb, who took it gingerly. "Just in case," Tag said grimly.

They put the groggy cub outside and Tag locked the door behind him.

There was no darkness quite as complete as being in the woods with only the moon and stars as beacons. The scent of wet pine and decomposing leaves made a musty perfume about them as they quickly stepped off the path to follow the thin beam of Tag's carefully shielded pocket light. Barbara stayed close, her fingers curled in Tag's belt so they wouldn't get separated in the blind trek through the forest. He moved at a steady jog, picking his way unerringly over obstacles that tore at her ankles and threatened to spill her to the mossy ground. Unseen branches and brambles sliced at the unprotected skin of her face, neck and hands, snagging her clothing as they pushed through the dense underbrush.

She didn't complain. She didn't break stride as they began to climb. Chet would expect them to take the easier routes in deference to Barbara's lack of skill. He'd be looking for them to head for the nearest landing via the shortest path. He wouldn't expect Tag to take her over a mountain in the middle of the night.

At least, that's what Tag was hoping. And by the time Chet figured it out, they'd have enough of a head start for it not to matter.

At least that was the plan. And it was working well. Tag had factored in all the possible variables... except one.

A weak sunlight filtered through the morning's rainy mist. Chilled, wet and exhausted, still Barbara had no objections to the pace. They took a few minutes to catch their breath atop one of the rugged peaks. They exchanged tight smiles. So far so good. But the funny thing about best laid plans relying on luck...

Tag went down with a howl of agony.

It took Barbara a long startled moment to realize he hadn't been shot. She knelt where he writhed on the ground, seeking the source of his pain. Finding it. Going blank with stark dismay.

He'd stepped into a poacher's trap. Cruel steel jaws had snapped his ankle like a pretzel rod. The evidence of that made her stomach heave mightily. Only the sounds of his distress kept her from losing her last spartan meal and called her back to cool thinking.

"Get it off. Get it off," he wheezed, rolling on the trampled leaves while trying to hold his leg still.

Girding her insides, she bent closer to examine the wicked device in horrified frustration. "How? I don't know how."

Conquering his out-of-control breathing, Tag eased up on his elbows to discover the worst. Bone jutted through the rip in his jeans and he was bleeding badly. Son of a bitch. He lay back, panting softly, digging up dirt with the furrow of his fingertips. Slowly, carefully, he explained the rudiments of the trap and how to release its awful hold on him, knowing once it was done, he wouldn't be much good for anything else. And so he told it to her straight.

"Once my foot is free, put a tourniquet on my leg and get the hell out of here."

"What?" She stared at him, not understanding.

"Go. I'll cover you for as long as I can."

He wanted her to run away while he lay broken, bleeding and alone to protect her flank.

"Nuts to that," she concluded flatly, dismissing his offer of sacrifice without a second thought.

"Barb—"

"Save your breath. This is going to hurt."

What an understatement. As she reached for the mechanism, Tag grabbed a sturdy stick and gripped it between his teeth, biting down upon the urge to scream when the trap's jaws opened and she eased his mangled ankle from its grasp. He continued to sweat and groan as she tied one of the stretchy sleeves from her jacket about his leg to stem the fearsome flow of blood. Then, as he thrashed weakly in a fog of pain, she found two substantial limbs to line up along his calf, binding them with strips from her other sleeve to stabilize his foot.

"Not bad for a city girl," she mused as she sat back to scrutinize her work. Tag's flailing hand grazed her hip. She caught it between hers, pressing fiercely. "You'll be all right."

"Go," was all he said before his eyes rolled up white, then closed.

Barbara continued to clutch his slack fingers, kneading them as she forced her thoughts from their paralysis. Go. How simple that would be. Think of herself first and let him take care of things. Hadn't that been her habit over the years? Stepping back from any risk to let another absorb it for her? Her family. Robert. Her son-in-law and daughter. And now Tag McGee. Wasn't it time for her take her own future in her hands to protect what she wanted to the limit of her life?

Leave him here to face the threat of Chet Allen?

Hardly.

A steady jouncing dragged him back to the edge of awareness. He had to ease up slowly to consciousness, lest the pain suck him back under again. He had the feeling he'd been drifting for far too long. Before he opened his eyes, he tried to make some sense of his situation. He was on his back but not on the ground. Glassy spears of hurt gnawed at his ankle as if the trap had yet to give him up. Heat baked through his insides even as he shivered fitfully. What the hell was going on? He attempted to speak. Wet his dry lips and tried again. A croak of sound escaped them.

"Barb?"

The odd movement stopped and his form went horizontal. Her palm fit to his cheek, cool in its caress.

"You're awake. I'm glad. I think we're almost there."

"Where?" He slit open his eyes to midmorning brightness and the glorious sight of Barbara D'Angelo's smile. It took him a long moment to wrest his gaze away to scan his surroundings. With some surprise, he realized they were almost on level ground.

What the hell?

She stood and he could see she was in her jog bra. She looked fit and toned and damned gorgeous. But why was she so undressed?

And then he realized he was clutching the tattered remains of her sweat jacket over him. She'd used his tough coat zipped around twin branches to fashion a crude but serviceable travois. With it, she'd hauled him down the mountainside while he was lost to fever.

Amazed, he drank from the bottle of water she offered him. She took a quick swallow, then recapped it while looking cautiously around for signs of trouble.

"Barb, what's going on?"

She regarded him with a patient smile. "You didn't think I was going to leave you behind, did you?

Yes. That's what he'd thought. That's what he'd told her to do. But here she was, like some glorious forest queen dragging his helpless butt out of danger.

Amazing.

"How far?"

He blinked, scrambling his groggy thoughts together to come up with an answer. He levered up slightly to look ahead to where they were going, gritting his teeth against the protesting agony of that move. He gestured feebly.

"Just up there. In that clearing."

Her hand touched to his damp brow. Her gaze was tender with concern. "Lie back and leave the driving to me."

He did so because he didn't have any choice. He couldn't get up and he couldn't take charge. So he swallowed his pride and trusted her to take care of them. His mind clouded up and by the time the overcasting fever lifted, he was situated at the crossroads of two trails, one leading to the water's edge and safety and the other to a well-used animal track. Barb smiled when she saw he recognized her.

"How are you feeling?"

"Like a bear bit off my foot. How about you?" he added more quietly.

"My personal trainer would be proud." She said that lightly but it didn't lessen the magnitude of what she'd done. Hell, he was proud. And surprised. And warmed by the strength of her commitment to him.

She'd come a long way from that naive teenager who clung to his heartstrings.

Basking in his appreciative stare, Barbara stood, planning to trot down to the boat landing to see if there was anything of any use in the small storage shed now that he could watch her back. She was pleased with her resourcefulness and with the fact that they were still breathing.

And then she turned right into the bore of Chet Allen's rifle.

"Hello, Barbie. You led me on quite a chase. Sorry to say game's over." She heard the click of the safety catch and his cold summation. "Nothing personal."

Chapter 14

After relieving her of her pistol, Chet looked around her to where Tag sat propped up against a tree. He scanned the roughly made splint dispassionately and shook his head.

"You'd have never stepped into a booby trap that easily in 'Nam."

"We're not in 'Nam anymore," Tag choked out.

Chet stared at him oddly for a moment then said, "I know. Don't you think I know that?"

"No, I don't think you do," Tag said quietly. "I don't think either of us came back."

Chet thought about it, then shrugged. "World's got no place for us old warriors."

Tag disagreed. "You're wrong, Chet. There's always a war someplace."

"That's where I'll be heading…as soon as this is done."

As soon as he'd killed them.

"Then Kelly wins."

Chet's eyes narrowed at Tag's flat summation, not liking it. Then he shrugged again. "Does it really matter?"

"It used to. It used to matter to the three of us."

Chet's features hardened. "Well we're not those stupid kids any more, are we, Mac? Robby, he turned on both of us, and you just up and left me out there to go mad. Why should I care what happens now?"

"Because it matters who makes the rules to those that follow them."

Chet stood motionless, seeming to consider that, and then he laughed. "You're wrong, Mac. I just don't care." The bore of his rifle shifted, centering on Tag's chest. Seeing his death coming fast, Tag tried to reach out to the friend he'd once known.

"Promise me you'll let Barbara go."

His icy gaze cut to the woman all of them had pursued with such zeal over a summer long ago. She returned his gaze steadily, not begging, not making a plea for her life.

Chet sighed regretfully. "Can't do that, not after she sees me put an end to you. It's going to be a tragic murder-suicide. Old lovers brought back together for an unhappy end. So sad." He hoisted the rifle. "I'd like to hash over old times some more, but I've got a plane to catch and I can't get on it unless you're dead. Sorry, Mac. Bad luck for you."

They could hear the low hum of a seaplane's engine. Chet's government escape from the island.

"Guess there's nothing else to say, is there?" Tag murmured stoically. And he braced for the bullet.

Just then, a rustling in the brush behind them distracted Chet. As he looked around to see what kind of threat was sneaking up on him, Tag brought his gun out from under Barbara's jacket. Catching the movement, Chet was quick to bring his weapon back to its original target. That's when Barbara grabbed the barrel and yanked it heavenward, giving Tag time to fire.

Chet glanced down in surprise at the feathered dart protruding from just below his collarbone. He gave a little laugh as he reached to pluck it out. Then abruptly staggered. Barbara wrenched the rifle from his hands and slammed the stock against his sternum, knocking him backward a few reeling steps. Then the ground opened up and he disappeared.

Tag leaned back against the supporting tree trunk. His vision was distorted and began to dim.

"Did we get him?" he asked in a curiously thick voice.

Barbara peered over the edge of the bear pit. Chet lay crumpled at the bottom, no threat to anyone for the moment. "Yes."

Tag closed his eyes. "He never would have stepped into a booby trap that easily in jungle, either."

"I guess that means we win."

Suddenly, she remembered the noise that gave them the chance to overcome him. She looked into the woods and gave an incredulous laugh.

"What?"

"You won't believe this."

Out of the brush wandered the hungry bear cub. It had been following after its only source of food and had ended up saving their lives. Weak with relief, Barbara broke off a piece of one of the power bars and fed it to their furry rescuer.

The roar of the seaplane grew louder, racing in tandem with that of a powerboat that was rapidly approaching the dock.

"That'll be Chaney," Tag muttered, losing his tenuous grip on alertness. "Go wave him in, Barb."

He let his attention wane until she returned with not just Jack Chaney but Patrick Kelly and several of his men. The plane circled once and headed for the horizon without its cargo. Chaney hung back, letting Kelly assume command.

Kelly directed his men to haul the unconscious Allen out of the pit and secure him with cuffs while he used a portable radio to call for an ambulance to meet them in Copper Harbor.

Tag just let it happen, too sick with pain to care who took control as long as Barbara was kneeling at his side. He exchanged another look with Chaney who gave one brief nod. That was all Tag needed to see before surrendering himself to a soothing darkness in Barbara D'Angelo's arms.

The bounce of the boat brought him back around. He was stretched out on a bench seat in the bow, his head on Barbara's lap. She was looking ahead, the wind and spray whipping her face and hair, making her look wild and free. She'd saved his life. But could she still save his soul?

Seeing his eyes open, Kelly came to squat down by him, his expression all encouraging camaraderie.

"My men will see to Allen. He won't be any trouble to anyone anymore."

They were going to kill him, Tag read between the lines.

"And I'm going to see you get the help you need, McGee."

They were going to kill him, too. A nice tidy cover-up.

Or at least that's what Kelly had planned.

The jut of the dock cut through the early mists. The throaty engine powered down so the boat could nudge up alongside the dock. Kelly tossed a rope to one of the shadowy figures waiting for them. With the mooring secured, Kelly's men hauled Allen up and passed him to the black-clad agents on the dock.

"Take him to the sheriff's station," Jack ordered as he came up behind Kelly. Kelly turned to him in surprise, not expecting to have his authority usurped. But then Chaney caught his wrist, snapping on a cuff and then quickly securing the other wrist, as well.

"What is this?"

"Justice," Chaney told him.

"What the hell do you think you're doing?" Kelly sputtered as he was handed up to the men who'd been waiting, freezing when he saw they weren't his men at all. "What's going on here? There's been a mistake."

"No mistake," came a quiet female voice from out

of the fog. Slowly, Kelly's wife stepped forward to regard him with loathing in her eyes. Behind her stood a man and a woman. Tag recognized the journalist from outside the Kennedy Center. He didn't understand.

As they were dragging Kelly down the dock, a gurney was hurried to the boat and the EMTs were quick to lift McGee onto it. As Jack was helping Barbara out of the boat, she saw the younger of the two Asian women approach the prone man to lift his hand and press it to her cheek.

"Thank you," she cried softly. "Thank you for what you did." She relinquished his hand reluctantly so they could rush him to the waiting ambulance.

Barbara looked to Jack for answers. But it was Su Quan Kelly who supplied them.

"Mrs. D'Angelo, these are my children."

She simply stared. She didn't understand, either. "I—I thought they were dead."

"So did I all these long years until my son saw the man who rescued them."

Jack cleared his throat and began to explain. "Mr. Quan found me when I was asking questions down in Little Saigon. He remembered McGee from the night his father was killed and his mother taken. McGee was supposed to have killed them, too, while Allen took their mother to where Kelly could stage a heroic rescue. The plan was for him to live happily ever after with a dead man's wife. Only McGee couldn't go through with it. He fired two shots so Allen would think he'd followed through on his orders. He wrapped the kids up in a rug as if he was disposing of the bodies only he took them to a neighboring village and left them with a nun in charge of the orphanage there. He gave her false names so Kelly wouldn't find them. He planned to come back for them to reunite them with their mother. Only—"

"Only Frye took his memory," Barbara concluded. "And no one, not even him, knew that they were alive or where he'd put them."

"It took us a long time to get out of the country after the Americans left," the journalist began. "Kelly took our mother with him as a war bride. It was years before we had the resources to look for her. Records were gone. Names were lost. But we remembered the soldier who saved our lives and when I saw him with the rifle Kelly planted in his hands after the shooting, I knew we had to do something to save his life, as he saved ours."

"Then Kelly shot Frye. How? How did Tag end up with the murder weapon?"

Jack supplied the answer once again. "Frye used a phrase to trigger them, to make them instantly open to suggestion. Frye thought Kelly was bringing McGee there to take out Allen, but he was the target all along. A falling-out of thieves, so to speak. Frye had become a liability to Kelly. He was going too public, bringing too much attention to himself and the past he shared with Kelly. Kelly got impatient waiting for Allen to act and figured he'd shut Frye up and get rid of McGee at the same time."

Jack caught Barbara's puzzled stare and said, "I found the right names in the notes your mother put together during the hypnosis thing. McGee gave them to her while he was under. Quan found me and after a few dozen phone calls, we put together this little farewell reunion tour for Allen and Kelly."

"Chet?"

"They'll make sure nobody gets to him before he has a chance to sing a pretty tune. And Kelly will be going away for a long, long time. After that..." He shrugged. He couldn't vouch for the government's plans for one of its best assassins.

"He killed my husband," Su Quan Kelly murmured. "I spent the last thirty years thinking my children had died with him. All those years, living a lie." Her voice was so low and raw with pain that Barbara couldn't help but go to her and offer an empathetic embrace. The two grown children came to take the weeping woman from her and they walked toward the shore, comforting one another. A family back together.

Jack put his arm about her shoulders, drawing her in tight. She glanced up at him with tears in her eyes.

"Thank you, Jack."

"Just seeing to my own."

She sighed, resting her head on his shoulder. Now to make Tag McGee a part of that intimate circle.

Chapter 15

The changing of shifts brought renewed activity to the hospital halls. Barbara straightened on the waiting-room couch, clutching the warmth of Tag's leather jacket to keep it from sliding off her shoulders. Her thoughts gathered slowly as she stretched and gave her head a roll to loosen the kinks. Jack had done everything he could to get her to go home, but she refused. She'd wanted to be here when Tag woke up.

The events of the previous day were still a blur. Because of the severity of his injury, Tag had been air-lifted to a downstate hospital as soon as he was stabilized. She and Jack had followed in the car. Even with her son-in-law behind the wheel breaking the speed laws and sometimes, she felt, the laws of gravity, it was after six in the evening by the time she rushed up to the information desk. The news wasn't good. Tag was still in surgery.

During the drive, Jack had filled her in on the details he'd discovered, but most of the information zipped by as fast and inconsequentially as the scenery. She didn't care about the *then* as much as she cared about the urgent *now*. Jack stayed with her long enough to see her situated at the hospital, but she could tell he was anxious to drive to a certain gym in a northern Detroit suburb to see what Chet Allen had left behind. Tag had passed him the key during the boat ride from the island with instructions to go there himself. He wasn't to trust anyone, either military or government. Jack had given his word that he'd see the evidence safely tucked away.

After learning of Tag's status, which was no news, Barbara shooed Jack on his way and then took her travel bag into the hospital bathroom to freshen up as best she could before beginning the all-night vigil. The surgery concluded after ten. The results were guarded, but she was given a promise by a compassionate nurse that they would have a better idea by morning. She couldn't see him until then.

So with her travel bag as a pillow and Tag's coat, which still carried his scent, as a comforter, she managed to snatch a few hours of rest. And between those brief restorative breaks, she thought long and hard about Taggert McGee.

She couldn't let him go again.

The moment they'd shared as teens was a wild,

sweet affair, testing the parameters of an adult love during a chaotic time. The promises they'd made to one another had been impossible to keep because of outside circumstances, because of their lack of maturity to handle an incredibly difficult situation. Their faith in one another hadn't survived the betrayals all around them. But that was the past.

She'd drifted through the years, comfortable yet not content. The something missing from her life was the spark Tag had ignited within a young girl's heart. She couldn't love Robert, not with that same deep passion, and he knew it. She hadn't blamed him for resenting that fact and she suffered for it, knowing he'd taken in the child of another man to raise as his own, knowing how hard he worked toward securing the future he'd vowed they'd share. Because she couldn't open her heart and soul to him, she gave him all her time, all her energy, so he might realize that dream of success.

Then Chet Allen's return snatched Robert's life and brought Tag back into hers. Tag McGee, with his spooky history of violence and fragmented memory. Tag McGee, with his tender touch, awakening her long dormant desires like a wildfire. Loving him had taught her about need and the heartbreaking pain of unexplained loss. Her willingness to make whatever sacrifices had been demanded to keep their child resurfaced now in her refusal to let him walk out of her life. He saw himself as a bad bet, as the trouble her family had warned of. Having Tag McGee was not going to be easy. There was plenty of work ahead to repair the fracture of faith between them. There was the damage done to his soul and psyche at the hands of those he'd entrusted with their care. She was no fool. Those gaps in his past couldn't be patched like potholes in a road. They'd require major reconstruction for that surface to be smooth again. But she wasn't afraid.

The only thing that scared her, the only thing that disturbed her rest, was the worry that Tag McGee would be unwilling to take the risk of loving her again. She'd failed him before, altering the direction their paths would take. They'd lived separate adult lives as strangers to one another. They'd reunited dragging along more baggage than a simple carry-on could contain.

What if he decided the effort to start over again was just too great this late in their lives?

She didn't know if her heart could stand it. But a deeper, stronger part of her knew she would. She'd survive. She'd go on for the sake of her family, working for Jack, spoiling her grandchild, doing her charity work while she put her emotions back in storage until the time Tag McGee was ready to confront what was between them. She could wait. She'd learned infinite patience. And she'd also discovered exactly what she wanted in life.

"Mom?"

She glanced up to see Tessa and her husband in the doorway. For once, there was no hesitation. Her daughter rushed across the room, bending to embrace her.

"Are you all right? How could all of this have been going on and no one said a word to me?"

Barbara smiled at the scolding and hugged her daughter tight. "It's over now," she promised wearily, then looked over her shoulder to Jack. "Isn't it?"

Jack's smile was thin and grim. "Allen may have been certifiable, but he sure knew how to keep records. Nothing wrong with his memory. Dates, places, amounts. Audio and videotape. A prosecutor's dream come true. Kelly's going down and he'll most likely take a few higher-ups with him."

"Good. You'll see to that, then?"

"Yes, ma'am." Then his smile took a funny quirk. "He's my father-in-law, you know," he said, referring to McGee.

Barbara slowly pushed Tessa back from her so she could meet her daughter's gaze. "And how do you feel about that?"

Tessa was a deep-thinking woman who hid her feelings well. Having spent a lifetime trying to earn the love of the man she thought was her father and never quite winning the acceptance she craved had put a strain on the relationship between mother and daughter. When Chet Allen had spilled Barbara's secrets on his way to jail the first time, Tessa had reeled away from the truth but had slowly come to an understanding of it. Forgiveness hadn't come quickly, although a new respect had been built between the two women. And now Barbara was asking her to open her heart to a stranger who'd shared a brief past and DNA with her mother thirty years ago.

"I'm not sure," was Tessa's painfully honest reply.

Barbara knew she couldn't ask for more than that

but tried anyway. "Will you give him a chance, Tessa? A chance to know you and Jack and Rose?"

"Is that what he wants?" So guarded, so accustomed to disappointment.

Barbara touched her cheek. "I'll ask him."

"I can, if he can," Tessa decided. Then she covered her mother's hand with her own, adding softly, "I can, if you can." Then she grinned unexpectedly. "And he'll be getting to know a new grandchild, as well."

Her startled gaze jumped between daughter and son-in-law. Jack's expression was impassive as he shrugged.

"I was just helping her get into some legal briefs and she took advantage of me." His dark eyes twinkled mischievously before settling on Tessa. Then his gaze positively glowed with love.

She hugged her daughter, murmuring tearful congratulations, at the same time thinking the last of her children had just grown up and away from her, starting a life separate from her own. As it should be. Her heart swelled with a poignant happiness for the journey Tessa and Jack were about to embark upon.

And Barbara wanted that same satisfying destination for herself.

It was like coming up from under water. Struggling against the pull and the desire to just drift upon the surrounding numbness for a while longer, Tag forced his eyes open and the first thing he saw was Barbara D'Angelo's tender smile.

"Welcome back."

"How—" He wet his lips and tried again. "How long have I been under?"

"Long enough to get a good night's sleep."

He took in her rumpled clothing and absence of makeup. "Doesn't look like you can say the same."

Barbara brushed her baby-fine hair back in a self-conscious gesture, a flush coming up her neck. She started to reach for her purse, for the repair kit of gloss and spray and concealer she kept there in case of emergencies.

"I must look a mess," she muttered anxiously.

"Considering what we've been through," he continued in the same gravelly voice, "you've got no right to look so damned good."

All the worries gusted from her on a single breath. She dropped her handbag and offered a weak smile. It was going to take some time to get used to being good enough as is. But she was looking forward to it.

"You don't look so bad yourself."

To her thinking, even with his hospital pallor and the bulky wrappings around his foot, he was fit and lean and the most desirable sight she'd ever beheld. No, he wasn't that tanned athletic youth with the shy smile and poetic soul. What he'd become was so much better. Deeper, more complex, confident. In all but one area.

He looked away from her adoring gaze, suddenly uncomfortable with her presence. What was she doing here? Come to say goodbye now that her family was safe and the threat over? He wouldn't blame her if she issued a cheery *adios* and a vow to exchange Christmas cards. After all she'd been through—the fear, the disappointment, the disillusionment—she shouldn't have to put up with his ghosts. But if she could...if she wanted to...

Barbara waited for his attention to turn back to her. He had that same guarded look she'd seen so often in her daughter's face. It had taken her far too long to deal with Tessa's uncertainties because of her own doubts and worries about rejection. She didn't have that kind of time where Tag was concerned.

Ticktock.

"The surgeon tells me everything went well," she began in a neutral tone. "You're going to have an extensive course of physical therapy to look forward to. Since there's no facility up in Copper Harbor, Jack was thinking that maybe you'd could stay at his compound and have a therapist visit you there."

"That's what Jack was thinking?" he echoed quietly. But what was she thinking? He waited, trying to suppress the very bad feeling that she was easing back out of his life.

"While you're there, you can get to know Tessa and Rose. You'll love Rose. She's such a dear. And Tessa. You won't believe how much the two of you have in common. You can field dress your handguns over coffee every morning."

He smiled narrowly, trying to whip up some enthusiasm. Though he wanted to get to know his daughter and her family, there was a more immediate situation he was interested in confronting first.

"Jack said since you'll most likely be bored after a week or two of getting soft watching daytime soaps with their housekeeper, he's got a group of would-be bodyguards he's training that you could pass a thing or two along to. If you want." Jack had looked at his dossier and had pronounced him a couple of rungs up the spook ladder over his head. Anything McGee had to teach was something worth knowing, he'd confessed.

"Sounds like you've got my plans all made for me."

She hesitated, not knowing how to read his impassive expression. His quiet statement gave nothing away. She took a breath and plunged on recklessly.

"Jack's been in contact with some government agencies regarding your…the other rehabilitation you need."

A cold, like freezing waters threatening to close over his head, seeped into Tag's spirit. He kept all signs of emotion from his face, but his eyes reflected that increasing chill.

"A handy guy to have around."

Seeing the distrust, the fear, shadowing his gaze, Barbara reached out to slip her hand over his, mindful of the IV tubes. His fingers remained still beneath hers. And cold.

"He spoke with my mom and had her check references on her end. These are top-notch professionals. They can help you sort things out. And they have security clearance…"

"So they can clean up the mess Frye made of my mind. And what's going to be left of me after that?

Anything useful or functional? Or will they just get in there and scramble things up to the point where I won't even know what the truth is? That Chet and I were windup killers? So that they can put me away someplace safe on the shelf next to Chet, along with all their other mistakes? To be locked away and forgotten?"

Her hand closed tight about his. "No. That's not what's going to happen."

"Barb, I know how these people work." He shut his eyes for a long moment and when he opened them, there was something else in the pale depths. A scary resignation. From someplace far away, he was hearing a soft sinister whisper. *Kingdom come.* Now he understood. Thy will be done. Not his will, but theirs. There was no use trying to fight them. Not if Barbara didn't want him to. "It's all right. They'll take care of me. I'm not your concern."

He was pushing her away, letting her make a graceful retreat. But that was the last thing Barbara wanted.

"The hell you aren't!"

He didn't move or react. His gaze locked on hers, watching the anger and passion build there into stormy gray waters.

"How dare you say that," she continued in a low, furious voice. "You think after all this, I'm just going to let you go and good riddance? You are mistaken, McGee. Why would you even suggest such a thing?" And then her umbrage blew over, leaving a calm that was disturbing rather than comforting. "Unless that's what you want."

When he didn't respond, she started to withdraw

her hand, only to have his fingers close tight, hanging on to that connection.

"I don't want to see you hurt anymore, Barb. I've brought nothing but pain to your life."

Her laugh was strained. "At least I've known I was alive. You call your daughter nothing? You call what we've shared together for these last few days—and nights—nothing?" She brought his hand up, pressing the back of it to the dampness on her cheek. "I'm not giving up on you, Taggert McGee. You are everything I've ever wanted and that has not changed. I want to help you heal, to help us heal. I'm not afraid of that. You're not Chet Allen. Or Robert. They couldn't tarnish the goodness in you. They couldn't push you over that line. And that's why I love you. That's why I trust you with my family, with my future. With my heart. Robert deceived us both. His selfish, jealous lie kept us from sharing a past. We can't change that. We can't go back, but we can go ahead. We can have that future, if that's what you still want."

He was motionless. He was listening. But was he believing?

What could she do to reassure him, to restore his faith?

"I love you."

In the end, that's all she needed to say.

"It's all I've ever wanted," he concluded softly. "It's all that's kept me going. The thought that maybe you'd kept that promise and were still waiting for me to come home. To come home to you."

Her heart turned over. Carefully, she leaned down to touch her lips to his, the gesture tender yet so very strong and sure. Then she pressed her cheek to his, feeling the hot dampness of tears, maybe hers, maybe his. Her words were thick with emotion when she told him one thing, softly, simply.

"Welcome home."

* * * * *

Design Tip of the Day

Ambience is everything. Imagine eating a foie gras at a luncheonette counter or a side of coleslaw at Le Cirque. It's not a matter of food but one of atmosphere. Remember that when planning your dining room design.
　　　　　　　　　　—Tips from *Teddi.com*

"Now that's the kind of man you should be looking for," my mother, the self-appointed keeper of my shelf-life stamp, says. She points with her fork at a man in the corner of the Steak-Out Restaurant, a dive I've just been hired to redecorate. Making this restaurant look four-star will be hard, but not half as hard as getting through lunch without strangling the woman across the table from me. "*He* would make a good husband."

"Oh, you can tell that from across the room?" I ask, wondering how it is she can forget that when we had trouble getting rid of my last husband, she shot him. "Besides being ten minutes away from death if he actually eats all that steak, he's twenty years too old for me and—shallow woman that I am—twenty pounds too heavy. Besides, I am *so* not looking for another husband here. I'm looking to design a new image for this place, looking for some sense of ambience, some feeling, something I can build a proposal on for them."

My mother studies the man in the corner, tilting her head, the better to gauge his age, I suppose. I think she's grimacing, but with all the Botox and Restylane injected into that face, it's hard to tell. She takes another bite of her steak salad, chews slowly so that I don't miss the fact that the steak is a poor cut and tougher than it should be. "You're concentrating on the wrong kind of proposal," she says finally. "Just look at this place, Teddi. It's a dive. There are hardly any other diners. What does *that* tell you about the food?"

"That they cater to a dinner crowd and it's lunchtime," I tell her.

I don't know what I was thinking bringing her here with me. I suppose I thought it would be better than eating alone. There really are days when my common sense goes on vacation. Clearly, this is one of them. I mean, really, did I not resolve less than three weeks ago that I would not let my mother get to me anymore?

What good are New Year's resolutions, anyway?

Mario approaches the man's table and my mother studies him while they converse. Eventually Mario leaves the table with a huff, after which the diner glances up and meets my mother's gaze. I think she's smiling at him. That or she's got indigestion. They size each other up.

I concentrate on making sketches in my notebook and try to ignore the fact that my mother is flirting. At nearly seventy, she's developed an unhealthy interest in members of the opposite sex to whom she isn't married.

According to my father, who has broken the TMI rule and given me Too Much Information, she has no interest in sex with him. Better, I suppose, to be clued in on what they aren't doing in the bedroom than have to hear what they might be doing.

"He's not so old," my mother says, noticing that I have barely touched the Chinese chicken salad she warned me not to get. "He's got about as many years on you as you have on your little cop friend."

She does this to make me crazy. I know it, but it works all the same. "Drew Scoones is not my little 'friend.' He's a detective with whom I—"

"Screwed around," my mother says. I must look shocked, because my mother laughs at me and asks if I think she doesn't know the "lingo."

What I thought she didn't know was that Drew and I actually tangled in the sheets. And, since it's possible

she's just fishing, I sidestep the issue and tell her that
Drew is just a couple of years younger than me and
that I don't need reminding. I dig into my salad with
renewed vigor, determined to show my mother that
Chinese chicken salad in a steak place was not the
stupid choice it's proving to be.

After a few more minutes of my picking at the
wilted leaves on my plate, the man my mother has me
nearly engaged to pays his bill and heads past us
toward the back of the restaurant. I watch my mother
take in his shoes, his suit and the diamond pinkie ring
that seems to be cutting off the circulation in his little
finger.

"Such nice hands," she says after the man is out of
sight. "Manicured." She and I both stare at my hands.
I have two popped acrylics that are being held on at
weird angles by bandages. My cuticles are ragged and
there's marker decorating my right hand from measuring carelessly when I did a drawing for a customer.

Twenty minutes later she's disappointed that he
managed to leave the restaurant without our noticing.
He will join the list of the ones I let get away. I will
hear about him twenty years from now when—
according to my mother—my children will be grown
and I will still be single, living pathetically alone with
several dogs and cats.

After my ex, that sounds good to me.

The waitress tells us that our meal has been taken
care of by the management and, after thanking
Mario, the owner, complimenting him on the wonderful meal and assuring him that once I have redeco-

rated his place people will be flocking here in droves (I actually use those words and ignore my mother when she rolls her eyes), my mother and I head for the restroom.

My father—unfortunately not with us today—has the patience of a saint. He got it over the years of living with my mother. She, perhaps as a result, figures he has the patience for both of them, and feels justified having none. For her, no rules apply, and a little thing like a picture of a man on the door to a public restroom is certainly no barrier to using the john. In all fairness, it does seem silly to stand and wait for the ladies' room if no one is using the men's room.

Still, it's the idea that rules don't apply to her, signs don't apply to her, conventions don't apply to her. She knocks on the door to the men's room. When no one answers she gestures to me to go in ahead. I tell her that I can certainly wait for the ladies' room to be free and she shrugs and goes in herself.

Not a minute later there is a bloodcurdling scream from behind the men's room door.

"Mom!" I yell. "Are you all right?"

Mario comes running over, the waitress on his heels. Two customers head our way while my mother continues to scream.

I try the door, but it is locked. I yell for her to open it and she fumbles with the knob. When she finally manages to unlock and open it, she is white behind her two streaks of blush, but she is on her feet and appears shaken but not stirred.

"What happened?" I ask her. So do Mario and the

waitress and the few customers who have migrated to the back of the place.

She points toward the bathroom and I go in, thinking it serves her right for using the men's room. But I see nothing amiss.

She gestures toward the stall, and, like any self-respecting and suspicious woman, I poke the door open with one finger, expecting the worst.

What I find is worse than the worst.

The husband my mother picked out for me is sitting on the toilet. His pants are puddled around his ankles, his hands are hanging at his sides. Pinned to his chest is some sort of Health Department certificate.

Oh, and there is a large, round, bloodless bullet hole between his eyes.

Four Nassau County police officers are securing the area, waiting for the detectives and crime scene personnel to show up. They are trying, though not very hard, to comfort my mother, who in another era would be considered to be suffering from the vapors. Less tactful in the twenty-first century, I'd say she was losing it. That is, if I didn't know her better, know she was milking it for everything it was worth.

My mother loves attention. As it begins to flag, she swoons and claims to feel faint. Despite four No Smoking signs, my mother insists it's all right for her to light up because, after all, she's in shock. Not to mention that signs, as we know, don't apply to her.

When asked not to smoke, she collapses mournfully

in a chair and lets her head loll to the side, all without mussing her hair.

Eventually, the detectives show up to find the four patrolmen all circled around her, debating whether to administer CPR, smelling salts or simply call the paramedics. I, however, know just what will snap her to attention.

"Detective Scoones," I say loudly. My mother parts the sea of cops.

"We have to stop meeting like this," he says lightly to me, but I can feel him checking me over with his eyes, making sure I'm all right while pretending not to care.

"What have you got in those pants?" my mother asks him, coming to her feet and staring at his crotch accusingly. "*Baydar?* Everywhere we Bayers are, you turn up. You don't expect me to buy that this is a coincidence, I hope."

Drew tells my mother that it's nice to see her, too, and asks if it's his fault that her daughter seems to attract disasters.

Charming to be made to feel like the bearer of a plague.

He asks how I am.

"Just peachy," I tell him. "I seem to be making a habit of finding dead bodies, my mother is driving me crazy and the catering hall I booked two freakin' years ago for Dana's bat mitzvah has just been shut down by the Board of Health!"

"Glad to see your luck's finally changing," he says, giving me a quick squeeze around the shoulders before turning his attention to the patrolmen, asking what they've got, whether they've taken any statements, moved anything, all the sort of stuff you see on TV, without any of the drama. That is, if you don't count my mother's threats to faint every few minutes when she senses no one's paying attention to her.

Mario tells his waitstaff to bring everyone espresso, which I decline because I'm wired enough. Drew pulls him aside and a minute later I'm handed a cup of coffee that smells divinely of Kahlúa.

The man knows me well. Too well.

His partner, whom I've met once or twice, says he'll interview the kitchen staff. Drew asks Mario if he minds if he takes statements from the patrons first and gets to him and the waitstaff afterward.

"No, no," Mario tells him. "Do the patrons first." Drew raises his eyebrow at me like he wants to know if I get the double entendre. I try to look bored.

"What is it with you and murder victims?" he asks me when we sit down at a table in the corner.

I search them out so that I can see you again, I almost say, but I'm afraid it will sound desperate instead of sarcastic.

My mother, lighting up and daring him with a look to tell her not to, reminds him that *she* was the one to find the body.

Drew asks what happened *this time*. My mother tells him how the man in the john was "taken" with me, couldn't take his eyes off me and blatantly flirted with both of us. To his credit, Drew doesn't laugh, but his smirk is undeniable to the trained eye. And I've had my eye trained on him for nearly a year now.

"While he was noticing you," he asks me, "did *you* notice anything about him? Was he waiting for anyone? Watching for anything?"

I tell him that he didn't appear to be waiting or watching. That he made no phone calls, was fairly intent on eating and did, indeed, flirt with my mother. This last bit Drew takes with a grain of salt, which was the way it was intended.

"And he had a short conversation with Mario," I tell him. "I think he might have been unhappy with the food, though he didn't send it back."

Drew asks what makes me think he was dissatisfied, and I tell him that the discussion seemed acrimonious and that Mario looked distressed when he left the table. Drew makes a note and says he'll look into it and asks about anyone else in the restaurant. Did I see anyone who didn't seem to belong, anyone who was watching the victim, anyone looking suspicious?

"Besides my mother?" I ask him, and Mom huffs and blows her cigarette smoke in my direction.

I tell him that there were several deliveries, the kitchen staff going in and out the back door to grab a smoke. He stops me and asks what I was doing checking out the back door of the restaurant.

Proudly—because, while he was off forgetting me, dropping by only once in a while to say hi to Jesse, my son, or drop something by for one of my daughters that he thought they might like, I was getting on with my life—I tell him that I'm decorating the place.

He looks genuinely impressed. "Commercial

customers? That's great," he says. Okay, that's what he *ought* to say. What he actually says is "Whatever pays the bills."

"Howard Rosen, the famous restaurant critic, got her the job," my mother says. "You met him—the good-looking, distinguished gentleman with the *real* job, something to be proud of. I guess you've never read his reviews in *Newsday*."

Drew, without missing a beat, tells her that Howard's reviews are on the top of his list, as soon as he learns how to read.

"I only meant—" my mother starts, but both of us assure her that we know just what she meant.

"So," Drew says. "Deliveries?"

I tell him that Mario would know better than I, but that I saw vegetables come in, maybe fish and linens.

"This is the second restaurant job Howard's got her," my mother tells Drew.

"At least she's getting *something* out of the relationship," he says.

"If he were here," my mother says, ignoring the insinuation, "he'd be comforting her instead of interrogating her. He'd be making sure we're both all right after such an ordeal."

"I'm sure he would," Drew agrees, then looks me in the eyes as if he's measuring my tolerance for shock. Quietly he adds, "But then maybe he doesn't know just what strong stuff your daughter's made of."

It's the closest thing to a tender moment I can expect from Drew Scoones. My mother breaks the spell. "She gets that from me," she says.

Both Drew and I take a minute, probably to pray that's all I inherited from her.

"I'm just trying to save you some time and effort," my mother tells him. "My money's on Howard."

Drew withers her with a look and mutters something that sounds suspiciously like "fool's gold." Then he excuses himself to go back to work.

I catch his sleeve and ask if it's all right for us to leave. He says sure, he knows where we live. I say goodbye to Mario. I assure him that I will have some sketches for him in a few days, all the while hoping that this murder doesn't cancel his redecorating plans. I need the money desperately, the alternative being borrowing from my parents and being strangled by the strings.

My mother is strangely quiet all the way to her house. She doesn't tell me what a loser Drew Scoones is—despite his good looks—and how I was obviously drooling over him. She doesn't ask me where Howard is taking me tonight or warn me not to tell my father about what happened because he will worry about us both and no doubt insist we see our respective psychiatrists.

She fidgets nervously, opening and closing her purse over and over again.

"You okay?" I ask her. After all, she's just found a dead man on the toilet and tough as she is, that's got to be upsetting.

When she doesn't answer me I pull over to the side of the road.

"Mom?" She refuses to meet my eyes. "You want me to take you to see Dr. Cohen?"

She looks out the window as if she's just realized we're on Broadway in Woodmere. "Aren't we near Marvin's Jewelers?" she asks, pulling something out of her purse.

"What have you got, Mother?" I ask, prying open her fingers to find the murdered man's ring.

"It was on the sink," she says in answer to my dropped jaw. "I was going to get his name and address and have you return it to him so that he could ask you out. I thought it was a sign that the two of you were meant to be together."

"He's dead, Mom. You understand that, right?" I ask. You never can tell when my mother is fine and when she's in la-la land.

"Well, I didn't know that," she shouts at me. "Not at the time."

I ask why she didn't give it to Drew, realize that she wouldn't give Drew the time in a clock shop and add, "...or one of the other policemen?"

"For heaven's sake," she tells me. "The man is dead, Teddi, and I took his ring. How would that look?"

Before I can tell her it looks just the way it is, she pulls out a cigarette and threatens to light it.

"I mean, really," she says, shaking her head like it's my brains that are loose. "What does he need with it now?"

Silhouette

nocturne™

**WAS HE HER SAVIOR
OR HER NIGHTMARE?**

HAUNTED
LISA CHILDS

Years ago, Ariel and her sisters were separated for
their own protection. Now the man who vowed
revenge on her family has resumed the hunt, and
Ariel must warn her sisters before it's too late.
The closer she comes to finding them, the more
secretive her fiancé becomes. Can she trust the man
she plans to spend eternity with? Or has he been
waiting for the perfect moment to destroy her?

On sale December 2006.

SNHDEC

In February, expect **MORE**
from

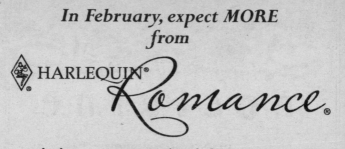

as it increases to six titles per month.

What's to come…

Rancher and Protector

Part of the

Western Weddings
miniseries

BY JUDY CHRISTENBERRY

*The Boss's
Pregnancy Proposal*

BY RAYE MORGAN

Don't miss February's
incredible line up of authors!

www.eHarlequin.com

REQUEST YOUR FREE BOOKS!

2 FREE NOVELS
PLUS 2 FREE GIFTS!

Silhouette® Romantic

SUSPENSE

Sparked by Danger, Fueled by Passion!

YES! Please send me 2 FREE Silhouette® Romantic Suspense novels and my 2 FREE gifts. After receiving them, if I don't wish to receive any more books, I can return the shipping statement marked "cancel." If I don't cancel, I will receive 4 brand-new novels every month and be billed just $4.24 per book in the U.S., or $4.99 per book in Canada, plus 25¢ shipping and handling per book plus applicable taxes, if any*. That's a savings of at least 15% off the cover price! I understand that accepting the 2 free books and gifts places me under no obligation to buy anything. I can always return a shipment and cancel at any time. Even if I never buy another book from Silhouette, the two free books and gifts are mine to keep forever.

240 SDN EEX6 340 SDN EEYJ

Name	(PLEASE PRINT)
Address	Apt. #
City	State/Prov.	Zip/Postal Code

Signature (if under 18, a parent or guardian must sign)

Mail to Silhouette Reader Service™:

IN U.S.A.
P.O. Box 1867
Buffalo, NY
14240-1867

IN CANADA
P.O. Box 609
Fort Erie, Ontario
L2A 5X3

Not valid to current Silhouette Intimate Moments subscribers.

**Want to try two free books from another line?
Call 1-800-873-8635 or visit www.morefreebooks.com.**

* Terms and prices subject to change without notice. NY residents add applicable sales tax. Canadian residents will be charged applicable provincial taxes and GST. This offer is limited to one order per household. All orders subject to approval. Credit or debit balances in a customer's account(s) may be offset by any other outstanding balance owed by or to the customer. Please allow 4 to 6 weeks for delivery.

SILRS06

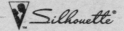

Don't miss
DAKOTA FORTUNES,
a six-book continuing series following
the Fortune family of South Dakota—
oil is in their blood and privilege
is their birthright.

This series kicks off with
USA TODAY bestselling author
PEGGY MORELAND'S
Merger of Fortunes
(SD #1771)
this January.

Other books in the series:
BACK IN FORTUNE'S BED by Bronwyn James (Feb)
FORTUNE'S VENGEFUL GROOM by Charlene Sands (March)
MISTRESS OF FORTUNE by Kathie DeNosky (April)
EXPECTING A FORTUNE by Jan Colley (May)
FORTUNE'S FORBIDDEN WOMAN by Heidi Betts (June)

SPECIAL EDITION™

Logan's Legacy Revisited

**THE LOGAN FAMILY IS BACK
WITH SIX NEW STORIES.**

Beginning in January 2007 with

THE COUPLE MOST LIKELY TO

by

LILIAN DARCY

Tragedy drove them apart. Reunited eighteen
years later, their attraction was once again
undeniable. But had time away changed
Jake Logan enough to let him face his fears
and commit to the woman he once loved?

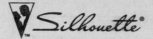
Silhouette®

COMING NEXT MONTH

#1447 THE BODYGUARD'S RETURN—Carla Cassidy
Wild West Bodyguards
When a reporter is attacked, her only hope is to hire bodyguard Joshua West to keep her safe. Together they investigate a series of alleged suicides and pray that they can overcome their desire for each other in the process.

#1448 HIGH-RISK AFFAIR—RaeAnne Thayne
FBI agent Cale Davis vows to protect a child who is a key witness in a drug-related murder…and realizes that the boy's mother has found a way to sneak through his hard shell to the vulnerable heart inside.

#1449 SPECIAL AGENT'S SEDUCTION—Lyn Stone
Special Ops
He has the contacts and the know-how. She has the government backing and the badge. Together they engage in a deadly game of cat and mouse to uncover stolen monies while warding off their sizzling attraction.

#1450 SHADOW HUNTER—Linda Conrad
Night Guardians
Will the past emerge and threaten Navajo tribal cop and warrior for the Brotherhood Hunter Long, when the only woman he ever cared for is kidnapped…and he's the only one who can save her?